"*I'm* the potential investor," **he said softly, "not my father."**

"That is not what I was told!"

A muscle knotted in Nick's jaw. She was staring at him through eyes so deep and blue they were almost violet. He'd stunned her, he could see that. Hell, he'd stunned himself.

"Trust me, Princess," he said in a voice as rough as sandpaper, "the only Orsini you're going to deal with is me."

Alessia Antoninni, Princess Antoninni, shook her head. "No," she said, and he silenced her the only way a man could silence a woman like this.

He thrust his hands into her hair, lifted her face to his and kissed her.

The patriarch of a powerful Sicilian dynasty,
Cesare Orsini has fallen ill, and he wants
atonement before he dies.

One by one he sends for his sons—
he has a mission for each to help him
clear his conscience.

His sons are proud and determined,
but they will do their duty—the tasks they
undertake will change their lives forever!
They are…

Darkly handsome—proud and arrogant.
The perfect Sicilian husbands!

by

Sandra Marton

Raffaele: Taming His Tempestuous Virgin
Dante: Claiming His Secret Love-Child
Falco: The Dark Guardian
Nicolo: The Powerful Sicilian

Sandra Marton

THE POWERFUL SICILIAN

the ORSINI Brothers

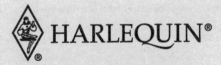

HARLEQUIN®

TORONTO • NEW YORK • LONDON
AMSTERDAM • PARIS • SYDNEY • HAMBURG
STOCKHOLM • ATHENS • TOKYO • MILAN • MADRID
PRAGUE • WARSAW • BUDAPEST • AUCKLAND

Recycling programs
for this product may
not exist in your area.

ISBN-13: 978-0-373-12959-1

NICOLO: THE POWERFUL SICILIAN

First North American Publication 2010.

Copyright © 2010 by Sandra Marton.

This edition published by arrangement with Harlequin Books S.A.

For questions and comments about the quality of this book please contact us at Customer_eCare@Harlequin.ca.

® and TM are trademarks of the publisher. Trademarks indicated with ® are registered in the United States Patent and Trademark Office, the Canadian Trade Marks Office and in other countries.

www.eHarlequin.com

Printed in U.S.A.

All about the author...
Sandra Marton

SANDRA MARTON wrote her first novel while she was still in elementary school. Her doting parents told her she'd be a writer someday and Sandra believed them. In high school and college, she wrote dark poetry nobody but her boyfriend understood, though looking back, she suspects he was just being kind. As a wife and mother, she wrote murky short stories in what little spare time she could manage, but not even her boyfriend-turned-husband could pretend to understand those. Sandra tried her hand at other things, among them teaching and serving on the board of education in her hometown, but the dream of becoming a writer was always in her heart.

At last Sandra realized she wanted to write books about what all women hope to find: love with that one special man, love that's rich with fire and passion, love that lasts forever. She wrote a novel, her very first, and sold it to the Harlequin® Presents line. Since then, she's written more than seventy books, all of them featuring sexy, gorgeous, larger-than-life heroes. A four-time RITA® Award finalist, she has also received eight *RT Book Reviews* awards for Best Harlequin® Presents of the Year and has been honored with *RT Book Reviews* Career Achievement Award for Series Romance.

Sandra lives with her very own sexy, gorgeous, larger-than-life hero in a sun-filled house on a quiet country lane in the northeastern United States.

Sandra loves to hear from her readers. You can contact her through her Web site, www.sandramarton.com, or at P.O. Box 295, Storrs CT 06268.

CHAPTER ONE

THE wedding at the little church in lower Manhattan and then the reception at the Orsini mansion had made for a long day, and Nicolo Orsini was more than ready to leave.

A naked woman was waiting in his bed.

She'd been there when he left his Central Park West triplex at ten that morning.

"Must you go, Nicky?" she'd said, with a pout almost as sexy as the lush body barely covered by the down duvet.

Nick had checked his tie in the mirror, checked the whole bit—the custom-tailored tux, the white silk shirt, even his wing tips, spit-polished the way he'd learned to do it in the corps. Then he'd walked back to the bed, dropped a light kiss on her hair and said yeah, he did.

It wasn't every day a man's brother got married.

He hadn't told her that, of course, he'd simply said he had to go to a wedding. Even that had been enough to put a spark of interest in her baby blues, but if he'd said it was one of his brothers doing the deed...

Talk about the Orsini brothers and weddings was not a thought he cared to leave bouncing around in any woman's head.

"I'll phone you," he'd said, and she'd pouted again—how come that pout was becoming less of a turn-on and more of an irritation?—and said maybe she'd just wait right where she was until he returned.

Nick lifted his champagne flute to his lips as he thought back to the morning.

Damn, he hoped not.

He had nothing against finding beautiful women in his bed, but his interest in this one was definitely waning and the female histrionics that sometimes accompanied the end of an affair were the last thing he wanted to deal with after a day like this. Much as he loved his brothers, his sisters, his mother, his sisters-in-law and his little nephew, there was such a thing as too much togetherness.

Or maybe it was just him. Either way, it was time to get moving.

He looked out the glass-walled conservatory at the garden behind the Orsini mansion. The flowering shrubs his sister Isabella had planted a couple of years ago were still green despite the onset of autumn. Beyond the shrubs, stone walls rose high enough to block out the streets of his childhood, streets that were changing so fast he hardly recognized them anymore. The Little Italy that had been home to generations of immigrants was rapidly giving way to Greenwich Village.

Trendy shops, upscale restaurants, art galleries. Progress, Nick thought grimly and drank some more of the champagne. He hated to see it happen. He'd grown up on these streets. Not that his memories were all warm and fuzzy. When your old man was the don of a powerful crime family, you learned early that your life was different. By the time he was nine or ten, he'd known what Cesare Orsini was and hated him for it.

But the bond with his mother and sisters had always been strong. As for the bond with his brothers…

Nick's lips curved in a smile.

That bond went beyond blood.

All day, his thoughts had dipped back to their shared childhoods. They'd fought like wolf cubs, teased each other unmercifully, stood together against kids who thought it might be fun to give the sons of a *famiglia* don a hard time. Barely out of their teens, they'd gone their separate ways only to come together again, their bond stronger than ever, to found the investment firm that had made them as wealthy and powerful as their father but without any of the ugliness of Cesare's life.

They were part of each other, Raffaele, Dante, Falco and him. Close in age, close in looks, in temperament, in everything that mattered.

Was that going to change? It had to. How could things remain the same when one after another, the Orsini brothers had taken wives?

Nick tossed back the rest of his champagne and headed for the bar that had been set up at one end of the conservatory. The bartender saw him coming, smiled politely as he popped the cork on another bottle of vintage Dom Pérignon and poured the pale gold liquid into a Baccarat flute.

"Thanks," Nick said.

Unbelievable, he thought as he watched Rafe dancing with his wife, Chiara. His brothers, married. He still couldn't get his head around it. First Rafe, then Dante and now even Falco. I-Am-An-Island-Unto-Myself Falco...

Absolutely unbelievable.

His brothers had fallen in love.

"So will you, someday," Rafe had said last night, as the four of them had toasted Falco's coming nuptials in The Bar, the Soho place they owned.

"Not me," he'd said, and they'd all laughed.

"Yeah, my man," Dante had said, "you, too."

"Trust me," Falco had said. "When you least expect it, you'll meet the right woman and next thing you know, she'll have your poor, pathetic heart right in the palm of her hand."

They'd all laughed, and Nick had let it go at that.

Why tell them that he'd already been there, done that—and no way in hell was he going to do it again.

Sure, it was possible his brothers would end up on the positive side of the grim statistics that said one in four marriages wouldn't last. Their wives seemed sweet and loving, but that was the thing about women, wasn't it?

They played games.

To put it bluntly, they lied like salesmen trying to sell ice to Eskimos.

Nick scowled, went back to the bar and put his untouched flute of champagne on its marble surface.

"Scotch," he said. "A double."

"I'm sorry, sir. I don't have Scotch."

"Bourbon, then."

"No bourbon, either."

Nick narrowed his dark eyes. "You're joking."

"No, Mr. Orsini." The bartender—a kid, maybe twenty-one, twenty-two—swallowed hard. "I'm really sorry, sir."

"Saying you're sorry isn't—"

A muscle ticked in Nick's jaw. Why give the kid a hard time? It wasn't his fault that the only liquid flowing today was stuff that cost two hundred, three hundred bucks a bottle. Cesare's idea, no doubt. His father's half-assed belief that serving a classy wine would erase the stink that clung to his name.

Forget that. Falco would have paid for the wedding himself, same as Dante and Rafe had done. That was the deal, the only way any of them had agreed to hold the receptions in what their mother insisted would always be their home. Isabella had done the flowers, Anna had made the catering and bar arrangements. If he wanted to bite somebody's head off, it would be hers.

That did it. The thought of taking on his fiery kid sister—either one of them, actually—made him laugh.

"Sorry," he told the kid. "I guess I only thought I was all champagned out."

The kid grinned as he filled a flute. "No problem, Mr. Orsini. Me, I'm all weddinged out. Did one yesterday afternoon, another last night and here I am again. Comes my turn, my lady and I are definitely gonna pass on this kind of stuff."

Nick raised his glass in a mock salute. It was the appropriate reaction but what he really wanted was to say was, *Hell, man, why get married at all?*

Still, he knew the answer.

A man made his mark in the world, he wanted to make it last. He wanted children to carry on his name.

So, yeah, he'd marry some day.

But he wouldn't pick a wife by fooling himself into thinking it was love.

Outside, visible through the walls of glass, the sky was graying. Rain, the weatherman had said, and it looked as if he'd got it right for a change.

Nick opened the door and stepped onto the patio.

When he was ready to choose a wife, he would do it logically, select a woman who'd fit seamlessly into his life, who would make no demands beyond the basic ones: that he support her comfortably and treat her with respect. Respect was all he would ask from her in return.

Logic was everything, in making business decisions, in planning a marriage. He would never make an emotional decision when selecting a bank to take over, or a stock to ride out. Why would he do it in selecting a wife?

Relying on emotion was a mistake.

Once, only once and never again, he had come dangerously close to making that error.

At least he hadn't been fool enough to tell anybody. Not even his brothers. He hadn't planned it that way; he'd just kept what was happening to himself, probably because it had all seemed so special. As a result, there hadn't been any "Oh, man, we're so sorry this happened to you" bull. Not that his brothers wouldn't have meant it, but there were some things a man was better off keeping to himself.

Things like learning you'd been used.

It had happened four years ago. He'd met a woman on a business trip to Seattle. She was smart, she was funny, she was beautiful. She came from a family that was as close to royalty as you could get in America but she'd made it in business on her own as the CFO of the small private bank he'd gone to the Northwest to buy.

To consider buying.

And that had turned out to be the key to everything.

She'd been in his bed by the end of the first day. And he'd wanted to keep her there. Before he knew it, they'd set a pattern. He flew to Seattle one weekend, she flew to New York the next. She said she missed him terribly when they weren't together; he admitted he felt the same way.

He had been falling in love, and he knew it.

A month into their affair, he decided he had to tell her about his father. He'd never done that before. A woman either knew his old man was a crook or she didn't. Who gave a damn? But this was different. This was—he'd avoided even thinking the word in the past—a relationship.

So, one night, lying in her bed, he told her.

"My father is Cesare Orsini." When she didn't react, he told her the rest. That Cesare was the head of a notorious *famiglia*. That he was a gangster.

"Oh," she purred, "I already knew that, Nicky." A sexy smile. "Actually, it's a turn-on."

A muscle knotted in his jaw.

The revelation should have set off warning bells. But the part of his anatomy with which he'd been thinking didn't have the luxury of possessing bells, warning or otherwise.

A long holiday weekend was coming. He'd asked her to spend it with him. She said she couldn't. Her grandmother, who lived in Oregon, was ill. She'd always been Grandma's favorite; Saturday morning, she'd fly out to spend the weekend with her, just the two of them, alone. She smiled. And she'd tell Grandma about the wonderful man she'd met.

Nick said he understood. It was a sweet thing to do.

And then, Friday night, he thought, what if he went with her? He could meet Grandma. Tell her how important her granddaughter had become to him.

He decided to make it a surprise.

He took the Orsini jet to Seattle, rented a car, drove to his lady's town house, took the key she'd given him and slipped quietly inside.

What came next had been like a punch in the gut.

His lady was in bed with her boss, the bank's CEO, laughing as she assured him that Nicolo Orsini was absolutely, positively going to make an offer for the bank that far exceeded its worth.

"An Orsini and you, babe," the man had said. "It's a classic. The princess and the stable boy…"

The delicate champagne flute shattered in Nick's hand.

"Merda!"

Champagne spilled on the jacket of his tux; a tiny drop of crimson oozed from a small cut on his hand. Nick yanked a pristine white handkerchief from his pocket, dabbed at his tux, at his finger…

"Hey, man," an amused male voice said, "the champagne's not that bad."

It was Rafe, coming toward him with a bottle of Heineken in each hand. Nick groaned with pleasure and reached for one.

"You're a miracle worker," he said. "Where'd this come from?"

"Ask me no questions, I'll tell you no lies." Rafe frowned, jerked his head at Nick's hand. "You okay?"

"Fine. See? The bleeding's stopped already."

"What happened?"

Nick shrugged. "I didn't know my own strength," he said with a lazy smile. "No problem. I'll get something and sweep it up."

"Trust me, Nick. One of the catering staff is bound to come out of the woodwork before you can—" A woman appeared, broom and dustpan in hand. "See? What did I tell you?"

Nick nodded his thanks, waited until the woman was gone, then touched his bottle to his brother's.

"To small miracles," he said, "like brothers with bottles of beer at just the right moment."

"I figured it would do away with that long face you were wearing."

"Me? A long face? I guess I was—ah, I was thinking about that Swiss deal."

"Forget business," Dante said, as he joined them. He, too, had a bottle of beer in his hand. "It's a party, remember?" He grinned as he leaned closer. "Gaby says that little caterer's assistant has been eyeing you all afternoon."

"Well, of course she has," Nick said, because he knew it was expected.

His brothers laughed. They talked for a few minutes and then it was time to say goodbye to the bride and groom.

Finally, he could get out of here.

He went through the whole routine—kisses, hugs, promises to his mother that he'd come to dinner as soon as he could. His father wasn't around. Perfect, he thought as he made his way down the long hall to the front door. He never had anything to say to Cesare beyond a perfunctory "hello" or "goodbye," and if the old man got hold of him today, it might take more than that because—

"Nicolo."

Hell. Think of the devil and he was sure to turn up.

"Leaving so soon, *mio figlio?*" Cesare, dressed not in Brioni today but in an Armani tux, flashed a smile.

"Yes," Nick said coldly.

Cesare chuckled. "So direct. A man after my own heart."

"You don't have a heart, Father."

"And you are quick. I like that, too."

"I'm sure I should be flattered but you'll forgive me if I'm not. Now, if you'll excuse me—"

"Have you forgotten you were to meet with me the day of Dante's wedding?"

Forgotten? Hardly. Cesare had cornered Falco and him; Nick had cooled his heels while Falco and the old man were closeted in his study and after a few minutes Nick had thought, *What am I doing, waiting here like an obedient servant?*

Besides, he'd known what his father wanted to tell him. Safe combinations. Vault locations. The names of lawyers, of accountants, everything the don felt his sons had to know in case of his death, when truth was none of them would ever touch the spoils of what the media called the Orsini *famiglia.*

"Five minutes," Nick said brusquely. "Just so long as you know in advance, Father, that whatever speech you've prepared, I'm not interested."

Freddo, Cesare's capo, stepped out of the shadows as father and son approached the don's study. Cesare waved the cold-eyed hoodlum aside, followed Nick into the room and shut the door.

"Perhaps, Nicolo, I will be able to change your mind."

Ten minutes later, Nick stared at his father.

"Let me be sure I get this. You want to invest in a winery."

Cesare, seated behind his oversized mahogany desk, hands folded on its polished surface, nodded. "Yes."

"The Antoninni winery in Florence, Italy."

"In Tuscany, Nicolo. Tuscany is a province. *Firenze* is a city within it."

"Spare me the geography lesson, okay? You're investing in a vineyard."

"I have not made that commitment yet but yes, I hope to invest in the prince's winery."

"The prince." Nick laughed, but the sound was not pleasant. "Sounds like a bad movie. *The Prince and the Don,* a farce in two acts."

"I am pleased you are amused," Cesare said coolly.

"What'd you do? Make him an offer he couldn't refuse?"

The don's expression hardened. "Watch how you speak to me."

"Or what?" Nick leaned over the desk and slapped his hands flat on the surface. "I'm not afraid of you, old man. I haven't been afraid of you since I figured out what you were two decades ago."

"Nor have you shown me the respect a son owes a father."

"I owe you nothing. And if respect's what you want from me—"

"We are wasting time. What I want from you is your professional expertise."

Nick stood straight, arms folded. "Meaning what?"

"Meaning, I need to know the true value of the vineyard before I make a final offer. A financial evaluation, you might call it."

"And?"

"And, I am asking you to make the evaluation for me."

Nick shook his head. "I evaluate banks, Father. Not grapes."

"You evaluate assets. It is your particular skill at the company you and your brothers own, is it not?"

"How nice." Nick's lips drew back from his teeth in a lupine smile. "That you noticed your sons own a business so different from yours, I mean."

"I am a businessman, Nicolo." Nick snorted; Cesare's eyes narrowed. "I am a businessman," he repeated. "And you are an expert on financial acquisitions. The prince offers me a ten percent interest for five million euros. Is that reasonable? Should my money buy me more, or will I lose it all if the company is in trouble?" The don picked up a manila envelope and rattled it. "He gave me facts and figures, but how do I know what they mean? I want your opinion, your conclusions."

"Send an accountant," Nick said with a tight smile. "One of the *paesano* who cooks your books."

"The real question," his father said, ignoring the jibe, "is why he wants my money. For expansion, he says, but is that true? The vineyard has been in his family for five hundred years. Now, suddenly, he requires outside investors. I need answers, Nicolo, and who better to get them for me than my own flesh and blood?"

"Nice try," Nick said coldly, "but it's a little late for the 'do it for Dad' routine."

"It is not for me." Cesare rose to his feet. "It is for your mother."

Nick burst out laughing. "That's good. That's great! 'Do it for your mother.' Right. As if Mama wants to invest in an

Italian vineyard." Nick's laughter stopped abruptly. "But it's not going to work, so if you're done—"

"There are things you do not know about your mother and me, Nicolo."

"Damned right, I don't. For starters, what in hell possessed her to marry you?"

"She married me for the same reason I married her." Cesare's gruff voice softened. "For love."

"Oh, sure," Nick said sarcastically. "You and she—"

"We eloped. Did you know that? She was betrothed to the wealthiest man in our village."

Nick couldn't keep his surprise from showing. Cesare saw it and nodded with satisfaction.

"That man is the father of Rafe's wife, Chiara."

"Chiara's father? My mother was engaged to…?"

"Your brother knows. He kept the information to himself, as is proper. *Sì,* Sofia and I eloped." Cesare's expression softened. "We fled to Tuscany."

Nick was still working on the fact that his mother had run away with his father, but he managed to ask the obvious question.

"Why? If you were both Sicilian…"

"Tuscany is beautiful, not harsh like Sicily but soft and golden. There are those in Italy who think Tuscany is the heart of our people's culture while Sicily and Sicilians…" The don shrugged. "What matters is that it was your mother's dream."

Nick felt the story drawing him in.

"Then, why did you emigrate to America?"

A small tic danced under Cesare's left eye.

"I had no skills other than those I acquired as a boy," he said in a low voice, "skills that had a use in Sicily. And here, in this country, as well. I knew this, you see, just as I knew that if I wanted to give your mother more than a life of poverty—"

Nick leaned over the desk and slammed his hands on either arm of his father's chair. "How dare you use my mother as an excuse for the things you've done!"

"I have done what I have done," Cesare said flatly. "The decisions were mine and I offer no apologies or excuses." His tone softened. "But if I could give Sofia this—this bit of Tuscan soil, this only thing she ever asked of me—"

"It's a hell of a story," Nick said coldly, "I'll grant you that."

But was it true? The only way to know was to ask his mother, and there wasn't a way in hell he was about to do that.

What it came down to was simple. Cesare might be using him…but so what? A couple of days out of his life was all it would take.

"Okay," Nick snapped. "I'll give you two days. That's it. Two days in Tuscany. Then I head home."

Cesare held out the manila envelope. "Everything you need is here, Nicolo. *Mille grazie.*"

"Don't thank me. Thank your wife for having eloped with a man unworthy of her forty years ago."

Nick took the envelope, turned on his heel and walked out.

"Two days, Alessia," Prince Vittorio Antoninni said. "That is all I ask."

Alessia Antoninni kept her gaze on the moonlit grape vines that stretched toward the softly rolling Tuscan hills. It was fall and the vines, long since stripped of their fruit, seemed lifeless.

"I told you, Papa, I have work waiting for me in Rome."

"Work," the prince scoffed. "Is that what you call running around with celebrities?"

Alessia looked at her father. They stood on the verandah

that spilled from the rear of the centuries-old villa that was her ancestral home.

"I work for a public relations firm," she said evenly. "I do not 'run around,' I deal with clients."

"Which means that handling public relations for your very own father should take you no effort at all."

"It is not a matter of effort. It is a matter of time. I don't have any."

"Perhaps what you do not have is the wish to be a dutiful daughter."

There were endless answers to that but the hour was late. Alessia decided to let the gauntlet lie where her father had thrown it.

"You should not have agreed to a visit from this American if you knew you would not be available for it."

"How many times must I explain? Something's come up. I cannot be here for *Signore* Orsini's visit and it would be impolite to cancel it."

"You mean, it would be dangerous to disappoint a gangster."

"Cesare Orsini is a businessman. Why believe the lies of the tabloid press?"

"Your staff can handle things. Your accountants, your secretary—"

"And what of the dinner party I arranged?" The prince raised an eyebrow. "Would you have my housekeeper assume the role of hostess?"

"I have not been your hostess for years. Let your mistress play the part. She's done it before."

"*Signore* Orsini was born in this country."

"He was born in Sicily," Alessia said, with all the disdain of a Tuscan aristocrat.

"And Sicilians often cling to the old ways. Being entertained by my mistress might offend him." The prince's eyes turned cool. "Did you expect me to deny that I have a mistress? You know of your mother's condition."

Alessia looked at him in disbelief. "My mother is in a *sanatorio!*"

"Indeed." The prince paused. "A very expensive *sanatorio.*"

Something in her father's tone sent a chill down Alessia's spine. "What are you saying?"

The prince sighed. "Without an infusion of capital, I am afraid I will have to make some difficult choices. About your mother and the *sanatorio.*"

"There are no choices." Alessia could feel her heart pounding. "There is the *sanatorio,* or there is the public hospital."

"As you say, my dear. There is the one—or there is the other."

Alessia shuddered. She knew he meant it. Her father was a man with no heart.

"I see the condemnation in your eyes, daughter, but I will not lose what has been in our family for five centuries."

"You should have thought of that before you brought the vineyard to the edge of bankruptcy."

The prince made an impatient gesture. "Will you do as I ask or not?"

Was there a choice? Alessia thought bitterly.

"Two days," she said. "That is all I can give you."

"Grazie, bella mia."

"A blackmailer does not thank the person he blackmails, Papa."

It wasn't much of a rejoinder, she thought as she went into the villa, to the room that had once been hers, but it would have to do.

CHAPTER TWO

THERE was no woman waiting in Nick's bed, but she'd left a note.

Call me.

Nick sighed and tossed the note aside. He'd call, but not until he'd returned from this pointless trip. Call, send flowers and say goodbye. It was definitely time to end things.

He stripped off the tux, showered, put on a set of well-worn Marine Corps sweats and went into the kitchen. It was a decorator's dream but he pretty much used it only for making a sandwich or a pot of coffee, as he was now, spooning the stuff into a French press, putting the kettle on to boil, then settling in to wait.

The more he thought about it, the more certain he was that he'd been suckered into going to Italy. That story about his mother... Even if it were true, and that was a stretch, why would his father have waited forty years to give her, as he'd put it, a little bit of Tuscany?

Not that it mattered.

He'd said he would do this thing. A man was nothing if he broke his word.

The kettle whistled. Nick made the coffee, gave it a few minutes, then poured some into an oversized mug. Too much champagne or maybe too much Cesare. Either way, a couple of sips and he felt the caffeine kicking in as he emptied the contents of the envelope his father had given him onto the polished stone counter.

He picked up a document, read a couple of paragraphs, then shook his head in dry amusement. He was due to meet with Prince Vittorio Antoninni the next day.

"Would have been nice if you'd consulted me first, Father," he muttered, but a quick meeting would serve his purpose. The sooner this was behind him, the better.

He drank a little more coffee, then reached for the phone. The Orsini jet was taking Falco and his bride on their honeymoon. No problem. The company used a travel agent; Nick had the guy's home phone number. It was one of the perks of doing seven figures worth of business with him every year.

To his surprise, there were no nonstop flights from Kennedy Airport to Florence. He would have to change planes in Rome. That meant the travel time would be longer than he liked, but still, two days for this would be enough. He arranged for a first-class ticket that would get him into the city by 2:00 p.m., arranged for a suite at the Grand Hotel and a rental car he'd pick up at the airport.

Okay.

Nick punched a speed-dial number, ordered *pad thai* from a little place a few blocks away. While he waited for it to arrive, he went through the rest of the Antoninni Vineyard papers, but he learned little more than he already knew. The Antoninni family had owned the land and the winery for five centuries. Prince Vittorio had taken over from his father; his daughter would eventually take over from him, though she seemed disinterested in anything to do with business.

Alessia Antoninni was a party girl. She called herself a publicist but she spent her time in Rome, running with a fast crowd of people too rich for their own good. He knew what she was like without half-trying. Self-centered. Self-indulgent.

And bored out of her empty mind. New York was filled with young women like her.

Not that it mattered to him.

His business was with her father. Without question, the sooner it was over with, the better.

There was a note in the envelope, on heavy vellum adorned with a royal crest. *Signore* Orsini was to telephone the prince's secretary when he knew the exact time of arrival. The prince would not simply send a car, he would, himself, be at the airport to greet *Signore* Orsini. And, of course, *Signore* Orsini would be his guest at the Antoninni villa in the hills outside *Firenze*.

Nick made the call. It was the middle of the night in Italy by then so he ended up leaving a voice mail message in what he suspected was terrible Italian because he'd never picked up more than the basics, confirming he'd be arriving the next day, as planned, but omitting the time and flight information, and politely refusing the offer that he stay at the villa.

He preferred being on his own when he was checking out possible investment properties.

The bell rang. It was the doorman with the *pad thai*. Nick settled down with his dinner and his laptop and went through the Antoninni Vineyards paperwork again.

By midnight, he had lots of questions and not many answers. He could only hope the prince could provide them.

The prince, Nick thought, and laughed. This entire thing was like a bad joke.

Alessia paced the waiting area in the Peretola Airport, the last of her patience rapidly fleeing.

This was like a bad joke, she thought grimly. If only she could see enough humor in it to laugh.

The Orsini gangster had left a voice-mail message in

the middle of the night. Did he not realize there was a time difference between America and Europe?

Probably not.

He was a hoodlum. He would have the IQ of a snail. The message was delivered in incredibly bad Italian. Delivered? Barked, was more like it, in Sicilian-Italian. Such a lower-class patois…but what else would such a man speak?

He had an interesting voice, she had to give him that. Low-pitched. Slightly husky. A young voice for an old man.

What counted was that the message was pointless. He would arrive today. Alessia bit back a snort of derision. Of course he would! That was the arrangement he had made with her father. Then there'd been something about hotel arrangements when he surely knew he would stay at the villa. As for his arrival time, the airline he was flying…

Nothing.

She'd had to waste time scanning for all the incoming flights that he could take from London or Paris or who knew where. She'd ended with a list of arrivals that ranged from early morning to this last one due in now, from Rome.

She had been pacing these grimy floors for hours. An entire day, wasted.

An unladylike word slipped from her lips. A nun, hurrying by, gave her a shocked look.

"You try putting yourself in my place," Alessia said to the nun's retreating back, and then she thought, *I am losing my mind!*

A message blinked on the arrivals board. *Grazie a Dio!* The plane from Rome had landed. Orsini had to be on it. Five minutes for the passengers to disembark. Ten for them to collect their luggage. Another ten to clear passport control…

Her feet were killing her.

She had worn Dior heels. Heels? They were more like stilts. Foolish to have done so but they went well with her ivory

Armani suit. She had dressed with care, not to impress this
Cesare Orsini but to remind him of who she was and who *he*
was and if that seemed wrong, so be it. Heaven only knew
what her father had led the man to think about this unholy
deal, but since going to work in Rome, she had seen enough
deals go sour to know that it was important to establish one's
position as soon as possible.

This gangster wanted to buy into the Antoninni Vineyards?
She would set the rules. That was her right, now that her father
had dumped the situation in her lap. And the first rule was
that if it had been left to her, the American thug would never
have thought to set foot on Tuscan soil.

Ah. Finally. The passengers from Rome were starting to
trickle into the hall. A trio of priests. A middle-aged woman,
wheeling a suitcase. Two teenaged boys with backpacks. A
harassed-looking mother clutching a wailing child. An el-
derly man, leaning on a cane. A young couple, hands tightly
clasped.

And a man.

Tall, dark-haired, impeccably dressed in what was surely
a custom-made suit, his stride long and fluid, the look on his
face one of such controlled anger that Alessia took an unthink-
ing step to her left.

A mistake, because he took one to his right.

They collided.

No. Too strong a word. His body simply brushed hers....

An electric shock seemed to jolt through her.

He looked at her. He must have felt the same thing, judging by the sudden narrowing of his eyes. Such dark eyes, the
color of the strongest, richest espresso. The rest of his features
were strong, too, she thought on a little inrush of breath. The
narrow nose, with just the slightest dent near the bridge. The
square jaw. The firm mouth.

It was a hard, masculine face. A beautiful face...

"Excuse me."

Alessia blinked. The man's voice was as cold and hard as his expression. And the words were a lie. "Excuse me," he'd said, but what he meant was, "Why don't you get out of my way?"

Her eyes narrowed, the same as his.

She took a step to the side. "You are excused," she said, her tone as frigid as his.

His dark eyebrows rose. "Charming," he muttered, and strode past her.

Charming, indeed. The rudeness of him! He had spoken in English; without thinking, she had answered in the same tongue. He was, without question, an American, and everyone knew how *they* were....

Wait.

Had there been something familiar in his voice? Deep. Husky. Silken, despite its sharpness...

A bustle of noise and motion jerked her back to the present. More passengers had just appeared. It was an interesting parade of humanity but when it ended, it had not included Cesare Orsini. There was no short, rotund figure wrapped in a dark overcoat, an old-fashioned fedora pulled low over his eyes.

To hell with this.

Alessia turned on her heel, marched through the terminal and out the exit doors. Her black Mercedes had acquired two more parking tickets. She yanked them from under the wiper blades, opened the car and tossed them inside.

Her father could deal with this nonsense.

She had had enough.

She got behind the wheel. Turned the key. Opened the windows. Started the engine. The Mercedes gave a polite but throaty roar. It had no effect on the pedestrians swarming past the hood. Crossing without acknowledging traffic was a game in Italy. Pedestrian or driver, you could not play if you showed fear.

Slowly, she inched the Mercedes forward. The crowd showed reluctance but, gradually, a narrow tunnel opened. Alessia pressed down harder and harder on the gas....

And struck something.

She heard the tinkle of glass. Saw the crowd part.

Saw the broken taillight of the Ferrari ahead of her.

Dio, what now? she thought as the driver's door flew open. A man stepped out, strode to the rear of the Ferrari—dammit, of all cars to hit, a Ferrari—looked at the shattered glass, then at her...

Cavolo!

It was him. The tall, dark-haired American. He didn't just look angry, he looked furious. Alessia almost shrank back in her seat as he marched toward her. Instead, she took a long, deliberate breath and stepped from her car, her professional easing-the-tension smile on her face.

"Sorry," she said briskly. "I didn't see you."

"You didn't see me? Am I driving a slot car?"

She almost asked him what a slot car was and caught herself just in time. All she wanted was to get home—to the villa, which was not really home but would have to do—and kick off her agonizingly painful shoes, peel off her wrinkled suit, pour herself a glass of wine...or maybe two glasses—

"Well? Do you have anything to say for yourself?"

His tone was obnoxious, as if this were her fault. It wasn't. He'd been parked in a no-parking zone. Yes, so had she, but what had that to do with anything?

"First you try to walk through me. Now you try to *drive* through me!" His mouth thinned. "Did you ever hear of paying attention to what you're doing?"

So much for easing the tension. Alessia drew herself up. "I don't like your attitude."

"*You* don't like *my* attitude?"

He laughed. The laugh was ugly. Insulting. Alessia narrowed her eyes.

"There is no point to this conversation," she said coldly. "I suggest we exchange insurance information. There has been no injury to either of us and only the slightest one to your vulgar automobile. I will, therefore, forgive your insulting attitude."

"My car is vulgar? My attitude is insulting, but you will forgive it?" The man glared at her. "What the hell is with this country, anyway? No direct flights from New York. A layover in Rome that's supposed to take forty minutes and ends up taking three hours, three endless hours because some idiot mechanic dropped a screwdriver, and when I made a perfectly reasonable attempt to charter a private plane instead of standing around, killing time…"

He was still talking but she couldn't hear him. Her thoughts were spinning. He had come from New York? A layover in Rome? A longer layover than planned?

"Do you speak Italian?" she blurted.

Stopped in midsentence, he glared at her as if she were crazy. "What?"

"I said, do you—"

"No. I do not. A few words, that's all, and what are you, an adjunct to passport control?"

"Say something. In Italian."

He shot her another look. Then he shrugged as if to say, *Hey, why not accommodate the inmate?* And said something in Italian.

Alessia gasped.

Not at what he'd said—it was impolite and it had to do with her mental state but who cared about that? She gasped because what he'd spoken was not really Italian, it was Sicilian. Sicilian, spoken in a deep, husky voice…

"Your name," she whispered.

"Excuse me?"

"Your name! What is it?"

Nick slapped his hands on his hips. Okay. Maybe he'd stepped into an alternate universe.

Or maybe this was the old-country version of Marco Polo. Kids played it back home, a dumb game where they bobbed around in a swimming pool, one yelling "Marco," another answering "Polo." It made about as much sense as this, an aggressive, mean-tempered babe—if you could call her a babe and, really, you couldn't—who had first tried to walk through him, then tried to run him down....

"Answer the question! Who are you? Are you Cesare Orsini?"

"No," Nick said truthfully.

"Are you sure?"

He laughed. That made her face turn pink.

"I think you are he. And if I am right, you've cost me an entire day."

"Meaning?"

"Meaning, I have been here for hours and hours, waiting for your arrival."

Nick's smile faded. "If you tell me you're Vittorio Antoninni, I won't believe you."

"I am his daughter. Alessia Antoninni." Her chin jutted forward. "And, obviously, you are who you say you are not!"

"You asked if I was Cesare Orsini. I'm not. I'm Nicolo Orsini. Cesare is my father."

"Your father? Impossible! I know nothing of a change in plans."

"In that case," Nick said coldly, "we're even, because I sure as hell don't know about a change in plans, either. Your father was supposed to meet me. If I'd let him meet me, that is, which I had no intention of doing."

"I have no idea what you're talking about."

"That makes things even. I don't understand anything you're babbling about, lady, and—"

"Where have you been all these hours?"

"Excuse me?"

"It is a simple question, *signore*. Where were you while I paced the floor here?"

"Where was I?" Nick's jaw shot forward. "In the first-class Alitalia lounge in Rome," he said sharply. "And trust me, princess, it loses its charm after a while."

"The title is no longer accurate."

Nick looked Alessia Antoninni over, from her falling-apart chignon to her wrinkled Armani suit to the shoes she seemed to be trying to ease off her feet.

"Yes," he said, "I can see that."

She flushed. "I was expecting—"

"My father. Yeah. I get that part. What I don't get is what you're doing here. Where are your old man and his driver?"

"So. You admit you knew that someone would be waiting for you. And yet, you left no word of your arrival time, of the airline you would be flying. You did not spend so much as a second looking for my father or his chauffeur inside the terminal, and you did not trouble yourself to telephone the villa when you did not see them. If you had, someone would have called me."

"Yeah, well, I'm sorry this didn't go according to royal protocol, princess, but life doesn't always do what you want."

"I repeat, I am not a princess. And this has nothing to do with protocol. If you had left your arrival information as part of that useless voice-mail message—"

"If I had, your father would have met me. Or, as it turns out, you'd have met me. And I'm not interested in being taken by the hand and shuttled to your villa while somebody tells me how lucky I am to be given the chance to invest in what's probably a disaster of a vineyard."

"I thought it was your gangster father who would be investing. And to so much as suggest the vineyard is a disaster—"

Alessia caught her breath as Nicolo Orsini stepped closer. With him this near, she had to tilt her head back to see his face. Even in these shoes of medieval torture, he towered over her.

"I'm here as my father's emissary," he said in a cold, dangerous voice. "And I'd advise you to watch what you say, princess. Insult one Orsini, you insult us all."

Nick frowned even as he said it. Where had that come from? Insult his brothers or, even worse, his mother or his sisters, and, of course, you insulted them all. But the old man? The don, who was part of something ancient and ugly and immoral? Was an insult to him an offense to all the Orsinis?

"Your father is what he is," Alessia Antoninni said with dogged determination. "If you expect me to pretend otherwise, you are wrong."

He looked down into her face. Her hair was an unruly mass of streaked gold, long tendrils dangling free of what had once been some kind of ladylike knot. Her eyes flashed defiance. There was a streak of soot on a cheekbone high enough to entice a man to trace his finger across its angled length.

The rest of her was a mess.

Still, she was stunning. He could see that now. Stunning. And arrogant. And she was looking at him as if he were beneath contempt.

His jaw tightened.

She had pegged him for the same kind of man as his father. He wasn't—but something in him rebelled at denying it. She was an aristocrat; his father was a peasant. Nick had once delved into the origins of *la famiglia,* enough to know that though some scholars traced the organization solely to banditry, others traced it to the rebellion of those trapped in poverty by rich, cruel landowners.

It didn't matter. Whatever the origins of his father's way of life, Nick despised it.

Still, there was a subtle difference between viewing that way of life from the comfort of America and viewing it here, on such ancient soil. It brought out a feeling new to him.

"Your father is also what he is," he said, his voice rough. "Or do you choose to forget that your vineyard was created by the sweat of others?"

"I do not need a lesson in socioeconomics! Besides, times have changed."

"They have, indeed." Nick smiled coldly. "You and your father must now come to me, an Orsini, to beg for money."

Alessia stiffened. "The House of Antoninni does not beg! And you forget, we come to Cesare Orsini, not to you."

She was right, of course. His only function was to report back to his father....

"Why, *signore*," she all but purred, "I see I have silenced you at last."

She smiled. It made his belly knot. There were hundreds of years of arrogance in that smile; it spoke of the differences between commoners and kings, and in that instant, Nick knew the game had changed.

He smiled, too, but something in it made her expression lose a little of its upper-class defiance. She began to step back but Nick caught her by the wrist and tugged her toward him.

"There's been a change in plans, princess."

"Let go of me!"

He did, but only to slip his hand around the nape of her neck. Tendrils of the softest gold tumbled over his fingers.

"I'm the potential investor," he said softly, "not my old man."

"That is not what my father told me!"

A muscle knotted in Nick's jaw. She was staring at him through eyes so deep a blue they were almost violet. He'd stunned her, he could see that. Hell, he'd stunned himself.

He might be a peasant, but he was also a man. And she was a woman. A woman who needed to learn that this was the twenty-first century, not the sixteenth.

Nick's gaze dropped to her lips, then rose so his eyes met hers.

"Trust me, princess," he said in a voice as rough as sandpaper. "The only Orsini you're going to deal with is me."

Alessia Antoninni, the Princess Antoninni, shook her head. "No," she said, and he silenced her the only way a man could silence a woman like this.

He thrust his hands into her hair, lifted her face to his and kissed her.

CHAPTER THREE

TIME seemed to stop.

Alessia was too stunned to react.

A stranger's powerful arms around her. His mouth on hers. The heat of his body, the leanly muscled male strength of it…

Then she gasped. Fury and indignation transformed her into a virago. She twisted her head, slammed her hands against his chest, knotted those hands into fists when he failed to let her go.

A mistake, all of it.

His hand slid up into her hair so that there was no way to turn away from his kiss. One big palm slid down her spine, stopped at its base and brought her tight against him.

Was he insane?

He was kissing her as if he had the right to do it. To take whatever he wanted because of who and what he was, and to hell with propriety or their surroundings or the fact that they'd met only minutes ago and already despised each other.

Her hands flattened against his chest again. She pushed at that wall of hard muscle and when that had no effect, she tried to squirm free.

Another mistake, worse than the first one.

Instantly, she felt the thrust of his aroused flesh against her belly.

Her heart thudded.

She began to tremble, and his lips moved on hers, the angle of the kiss changing so that she had to tilt her head back. Was that why she suddenly felt dizzy and the ground took a delicate tilt beneath her feet?

She heard a sound. Was it she who'd made it, an almost imperceptible whimper overlaid by Nicolo Orsini's raw, ragged groan?

Her hands moved. Slid to his shoulders. Into his hair. Her lips began to part….

And then it was over.

He clasped her arms with such force that her eyes flew open, and as they did, he set her away from him.

She stared at him. His face was all harsh planes and angles; his eyes were slits of obsidian beneath thick, black lashes. Faint stripes of color ran beneath his high cheekbones as a muscle ticked in his jaw.

Alessia wanted to slap his face. More than that, she wanted to run.

But she wouldn't. She knew better than to show fear to a predatory animal. It was a lesson she'd learned when she was twelve, hiking the golden Tuscan hills alone late one afternoon and suddenly coming face-to-face with an enormous wild boar. Its long, razor-sharp tusks could easily have torn her open.

Despite her terror, she'd stood her ground. After what had seemed an eternity, the creature had snorted, stepped back and faded into the brush.

Now, as then, she forced herself to stand still. Not only wild animals but men, too, measured power in the fear they could engender.

That was why Nicolo Orsini had kissed her, and why she would not run from him. Instead, she drew a steadying breath and then slowly, deliberately, wiped the back of her hand across her mouth.

"If that was meant to impress me," she said in a steady voice, "it failed in its purpose."

The slightest smile curved his mouth.

"Did it," he said.

His tone made it clear the words were not a question. Alessia decided to ignore the implications.

"And I warn you, *signore,* if you do anything like that again—"

"Spare me the threats. You're in no position to make any."

Dio, the man was hateful! Alessia's chin lifted. *"Sei un barbaro!"*

"I'm a barbarian, huh?" He grinned. "Come on, sugar. Don't hold back. Say what you're thinking." His phony smile vanished. "What I am is the man who holds the purse strings. Remember that and we'll get along just fine."

Alessia stared at the hateful American and the last of her composure slipped away.

"We will not get along at all, *signore.* There has been a change in plans. The Antoninni Vineyard is not available for investment. You have made a long trip for nothing."

Nick narrowed his eyes. The *principessa* stood tall, shoulders back, head lifted in an attitude of defiance. She despised him, which was fine. He didn't think any better of her. All that was clear and up-front. The only question was, why had he kissed her?

To put her in her place?

A lie.

He didn't deal with women that way. He had faults, sure, but using sex as a weapon wasn't one of them. And he was not a man who'd ever take anything a woman wasn't eager to give.

Aside from all that, if putting her in her place had been what he'd intended, it had backfired. She wasn't shaken by what had happened; she was as cold and disapproving as ever. He must have imagined that something had changed in the last seconds of that kiss. That her mouth had softened. That her body had yielded to his. That she had parted her lips for him, that she had moaned…

Or had the moan been his?

"Do you understand me, *Signore* Orsini? Go home. Go back to your people. You have no further business here."

Nick looked at her. The message was clear. He was not only a barbarian, but he was also a Sicilian thug. An Orsini. And that was more than sufficient for a woman like her.

"We shall, of course, reimburse you for any expenses you've incurred."

The imperial *we*. The princess, addressing one of her subjects. Nick smiled, folded his arms and leaned back against the side of the Ferrari. It was a smile that those who'd faced him in boardroom battles or desert combat would have known enough to fear.

Hell, he thought coldly, *why not live down to her expectations?*

"Such a generous offer," he said softly.

"Yes. It is." She shot a look at the Ferrari's bumper. "I see some simple damage. Send us the bill."

"Shall I send it at the same time I send you a list of…how did you put it? The expenses I've incurred?"

"As you prefer. And now, *signore*…"

"And now, you assume, *arrivederci*."

"Assume?" she said, her tone one of elegant disdain.

But she didn't look elegant. Nick's gaze made a slow circuit again, from the shoes that seemed to make her wobble to the wrinkled silk suit to the drawn-back hair. Wispy strands the color of winter sunlight fell around her oval face.

There was a bedraggled look about her.

And maybe *bedraggled* was the right word.

She looked as if she'd just tumbled out of a man's bed. His bed, he thought, and felt the immediate response of his body to the image of what it would be like to strip the arrogant princess of her clothes and do whatever it took to turn all that frosty hauteur to hot passion.

He did a mental double take. Why would he even think of something like that? Alessia Antoninni was beautiful in the way statues were beautiful. There was nothing soft or warm or welcoming about her. She wasn't a challenge, she was a turnoff. That he'd even imagined bedding her—hell, that he'd actually kissed her—made him furious.

Dammit, he thought, and he took his anger and put it where it rightly belonged.

"You were right," he said brusquely, "my trip was lengthy. Eight hours flying to Rome from New York, then a three-hour delay at the airport added up to lots of time to kill."

"And you expect compensation for that time immediately."

She said it as if it were a given. Nick watched as she opened her purse, rummaged through it and finally extracted a checkbook. "If you can provide me with a figure—"

She gasped as his hand closed around her wrist. His fingers were biting into her flesh. He was probably going to mark that tender, upper-class skin. Not only didn't he give a damn, but he was also grimly pleased to do it.

"Are you always so sure of yourself, princess? Or is it only with me?"

Her eyes flashed.

"Let go of me, Mr. Orsini."

Nick smiled tightly. "What happened to *signore?* Don't I even rate that much now that I'm about to call your bluff?"

"I don't know what you're talking about. And if you don't unhand me—"

"Another threat, *principessa?*" His smile twisted. "Maybe you need to listen before you make threats."

"Listen to what?" She looked as if she wanted to kill him. Fine, he thought grimly. The more certain she was of herself, the more he'd enjoy the sight of her taking a metaphoric tumble right on her icy ass. His grasp on her tightened until they were a breath apart. "I repeat, I had lots of time on my hands. I spent it going through the material your father sent about your precious vineyard. It was detailed. Very detailed… but there was lots missing."

"I have no knowledge of what material you saw and it is of no interest to me. You are—"

"Dismissed? A while ago, I was excused. Now I'm dismissed." Nick's smile was as frigid as his tone. "Antoninni Vineyards is on the verge of ruin."

"That is not your concern."

"Four years of bad weather damaged the grapes. Your old man chose new plantings that turned out to be a mistake. He made lousy marketing decisions. I don't know a damned thing about viniculture—"

"How nice to hear you admit it."

"But I do know about investments. I added up some figures, added them up again and figured out, real fast, that what your father neglected to list in that report is at least as meaningful as what he did."

"I don't know what you're talking about," she said, but Nick could hear the lie in the words.

"I think you do. Papa Prince took more cash out of those vineyards than he put in. Where did it go, sugar? The horses? The casinos? Women?"

Alessia yanked furiously on her imprisoned hand. "This conversation is over!"

"Without money—and we both know it's going to require more than the five million euros Daddy requested—without it, your family's business will be a thing of the past."

"You are a fine one to talk about family businesses," she said, her face filling with color.

It was a nicely placed jibe. Dead wrong, but she had no way of knowing that and Nick had no interest in pointing it out. She thought he was a *famiglia* heavy? Let her think it. Hell, he wanted her to think it. There was a sweet pleasure in a woman like this believing she was on the receiving end of help from the man she believed him to be.

"The bottom line," he said, "is that you need my money. I'd bet my last dollar your father will be more than happy to remind you of that."

"I need nothing from a man such as you!"

"Five hundred years of royal living, gone in the blink of an eye?"

"Do you think that matters to me?"

"I think it matters enough so that you were willing to show up today to greet a commoner."

"You're wrong, Mr. Orsini. I only, as you put it, showed up today because—because—"

She blinked. Nick could almost see her processing what was happening. She'd been sent to greet him. She was the prince's reception committee. She was an Antoninni, unaccustomed to dealing with the peasants, but she didn't have the power to get rid of him.

No wonder she was staring at him as if she'd just remembered something she'd all but forgotten.

He was sure he knew what that "something" was.

The princess had been flexing muscle she didn't have. She had no power. To all intents, she might as well have been a chauffeur, sent to meet the plane of the visiting banker.

"What's the problem?" Nick smiled thinly. "Thinking twice

about telling me to leave?" When she didn't answer, he took his cell phone from his pocket and offered it to her. "Here. Call Daddy. See what he says about sending me home."

Alessia looked at the sleek bit of plastic as if it might bite her. Then she looked at the man holding it toward her.

Bastardo insolente!

He knew damned well she wasn't about to make that call. He just didn't know why.

Mama, she thought, *Mama, how could I have forgotten you?*

For a few moments, anger at this horrible man had blinded her to reality. Now, it was back. She'd made a bargain with the devil. If she wanted her mother to remain in the *sanatorio,* she could not get rid of Nicolo Orsini. She had to deal with him, no matter what.

He was vile.

His macho arrogance. His brutal occupation, if you could call being a hoodlum an occupation. And that kiss, the assumption that he was irresistible, that the male domination of his world extended to hers...

Vile was not a strong enough word.

It didn't matter.

She was stuck with him. He was her problem, and she knew how to handle that. Problems were her specialty. Let her father think that the public relations business was nothing but an excuse for protecting people with too much money and ego. Perhaps that was a reflection of what he knew of Rome and Romans.

That was not her world.

Alessia had put endless days, weeks and months into learning how to deal with the people her firm represented.

Having a royal title helped, though she loathed the idea that titles should exist at all in today's complex world. The rest? Damned hard work.

Preventing clients from making asses of themselves was part of what she did. Cleaning up after they'd done so anyway was another part, as was making sure they did what they were supposed to do without veering from an accepted plan.

Some clients were pleasant, talented people. Some were not. And still some, admittedly a small percentage, thought that money and power and, often, good looks made them gods.

There was no question as to which category Nicolo Orsini belonged, nor was there any question that she could handle him. The truth was, given the circumstances, she had no choice.

"A problem, princess? Have you forgotten Daddy's phone number?"

She blinked, looked up at him. Barbarian though he was, gangster that he was, Nicolo Orsini was also—there was no other word for it—magnificent. The epitome of masculinity. Alessia met a lot of very good-looking men in her work. Actors, industrialists, men whose money bought them the clothes, the cars that could turn a nice-looking man into a good-looking one.

The American's clothes were obviously expensive, his haircut as well. But he was also—could you call a man *gorgeous?* Because that was what he was. Gorgeous, and it was not what he wore or how he was groomed.

It was him.

The thick, espresso-brown hair. The eyes the color of night, the strong, straight nose set above a firm mouth and chiseled jaw. Even that little depression between nose and mouth, what was it called? A philtrum. That was it. How could something with such a foolish name be sexy?

The truth was, all of him was sexy. The long, leanly muscled body. The hard face. The sculpted lips. Perfect in design, in texture. She knew that. Knew the warmth of that mouth, the feel of it against hers. If she'd parted her own lips a little when he'd kissed her, she'd even know his taste…

"Take a good look, princess. Let me know if you like what you see."

Alessia's gaze flew to his. His tone was as insulting as the heat in his eyes.

She felt her face redden.

That she could find him physically attractive was shocking. She didn't understand it. A man's looks meant nothing; she had never been taken in by such superficial things. No matter. Living with her father, dealing with his careless verbal and emotional cruelty, had taught her the benefits of a quick recovery.

"I was thinking," she said coolly, "that you do not look like a savage, *Signore* Orsini, but that only proves that looks can be deceiving."

He hesitated. Then, he shrugged.

"Your father is what he is, as is mine, *principessa*. As for me—I am precisely what you see."

Alessia's eyebrows rose. It was, at first, a disconcerting answer. Then she realized he was simply saying that she was right. He was the son of a don, a man from his father's world, venerated in some dark corners of old Sicily but despised by decent Italians everywhere.

And yes, she would have to deal with him.

So. A tour of the vineyard tomorrow. The formal dinner tomorrow night. He'd be gone the following day, out of her life, forever.

She could manage that.

As for what her father had intended, that she act as Orsini's driver, that he stay at the villa… Out of the question. He'd made it easy. He'd already told her he preferred to be on his own. The Ferrari, which would be a rental, was proof of it. Good. Excellent. As for his being a guest at the villa—she would suggest a hotel, if he hadn't already arranged for one, and pick him up there in the morning.

Easier and easier, she thought, but before she could say anything, Orsini punched a button on his cell phone and began speaking in English. There was no mistaking the conversation. He was talking with the agency from which he'd rented the Ferrari, telling a clerk in brisk tones of command that they could pick up the car here, at the curb. There was some minor damage; they could contact his insurance company. No, the car was fine except for that. It was simply that he would not need a car, after all.

"But of course you'll need it," Alessia blurted. "To drive to your hotel. You did make hotel reservations, didn't you?"

He smiled tightly. Eyes still locked to hers, he hit another button on his phone. She listened as he canceled a reservation at the Grand. Then he flipped the phone closed.

"Your father intended that I stay at your villa and that you be my tour guide. Isn't that right, princess?"

"Don't call me that!"

"It's what you are, isn't it? The princess who commands the peasants?"

Alessia thought of responding, then thought better of it. Instead, she jerked her head toward her Mercedes, still just behind the Ferrari.

"Get in," she said brusquely.

"Such a warm and hospitable invitation."

She strode around the car, got behind the wheel, sat stiffly as he folded his long legs under the dashboard. Then she slammed the car into gear, backed up just enough to avoid hitting the Ferrari again and pulled into traffic.

"Two days," she said through gritted teeth.

"Sorry?"

Dio, she hated him! The pleasant tone, the polite manner that was about as real as…as fairies at the bottom of the garden. Ahead, a green light turned red. She slowed the Mercedes, pulled to the light and stopped.

"I said, I can give you two days. That's more than enough time for you to tour the vineyard, see the wine-making operation and meet with my father's managerial staff."

Nick found the control next to his seat, pushed it and eased the seat farther back. Two days had been exactly the amount of time he'd intended to be in Tuscany...but things had changed.

"Really," he drawled. "Two days, hmm?"

"Two days," Alessia repeated briskly. "As I said, that's more than sufficient time to—"

"Two weeks," he said. "I'll need that much time to make a decision. And, of course, I'll expect you to be available to me 24/7."

She looked at him. The look of disbelief on her face made him want to laugh, especially considering that he'd just changed all the plans he'd so carefully made but, dammit, the woman needed to be taught a lesson in humility.

"Are you *pazzo?* There is no way in hell I am going to endure two weeks of—"

Nick leaned over. Put his mouth on hers. Kissed her, and when she tried to jerk away, he curved his hand around her jaw and went on kissing her until she made a little sound and when she did, he parted her lips with his, bit lightly into the exquisite softness of her bottom lip...

A horn honked impatiently behind them.

Nick let go of Alessia and sat back.

"Two weeks," he said in a gruff voice. "If you want that money badly enough, that's how long it's going to take to get it."

He folded his arms and stared straight ahead. He could feel her eyes on him. The horn behind them beeped again, this time joined by a growing chorus.

Alessia exploded, said the word that had horrified the nun at the airport but only made him laugh.

Then she stepped on the gas and the Mercedes all but flew down the highway.

CHAPTER FOUR

NICK was not a man who enjoyed letting someone else take the wheel of a car.

Life was all about control. It was a lesson all Cesare's sons had learned.

You could count on a microphone or a camera being shoved in your face anytime your old man hit the news and the only way to deal with the idiots who thought it was okay to invade your privacy was to keep your mouth shut and maintain your self-control.

The simple practice had served him well, not just on the streets of Little Italy but in the war zones where he'd seen action as a marine and, more recently, in the plush boardrooms where he negotiated billion-dollar deals. He'd never thought much about how his reliance on self-control impacted other parts of his life but now, sitting beside Alessia Antoninni as she drove the Mercedes along a busy highway, he knew he was in trouble.

They'd been on the road for maybe twenty minutes. Twenty more, and Nick figured he was either going to put a hole through the floorboard from constantly trying to stamp on a brake pedal that didn't exist or maybe he'd just pluck the princess from behind the steering wheel and take over.

She was, what, twenty-five? Twenty-six?

He looked at her, the stony profile, the set mouth, the fists gripping the steering wheel. It was too dark by now to see but he'd have bet a bundle her knuckles were white.

Whatever her age, she had a long way to go before she'd qualify for all those jokes that began, "There's this little old lady driving down a highway…"

Forget that. He had an aunt who was eighty-five. Even she didn't drive like this. Besides, he was long past being amused. What he was rapidly working up to was being scared spitless.

Not a good thing for a man who had never come up against anything he truly feared.

Until now.

Until this.

Alessia had managed to push the speed to a dazzling twenty miles an hour when the other cars were whipping by at one hundred. Okay, so that was an exaggeration. Maybe the others were doing ninety and she was doing half that. The point was, she was a road hazard.

Either she didn't know it or she didn't give a damn.

Cars zoomed up behind them, horns blasting. Swerved by them, and because the princess favored staying in the center lane, there was lots of opportunity for drivers passing on the right to put down their windows and scream the necessary invectives, complete with accompanying hand gestures.

And yes, it seemed as if the same one-fingered salute that worked in Manhattan worked equally well in Tuscany.

Alessia, oblivious, drove on.

Okay, Nick thought grimly, okay, there had to be something he could say. Or do. Carefully, searching for the right words, he cleared his throat.

"Ah, is something wrong with the car?" He waited a beat. "I mean, if that's the reason you're going so slow—"

"I am at the proper speed."

"Yeah, well, actually, I don't think you are."

"Actually," she said coldly, "I do not care what you think."

So much for subtlety. "Actually," Nick said, emphasizing the word, "I'm certain that you don't. What I'm trying to tell you, politely, is that it's a mistake not to keep up with traffic."

"The mistake is that of the traffic."

"The mistake is that of the traffic?"

"That is what I said. This is the proper speed for the hour and the road conditions."

"What conditions? The weather's fine. The road's smooth and straight. Traffic's moving the way it should except for—"

"*I* am driving, Mr. Orsini. Not you."

Mr. Orsini. She was even more angry than before; he'd already figured out that her mood dictated whether he was "mister" or *"signore."*

"Yes. You are. But—"

A big truck flew past them, so close he could have reached out and touched it. Nick found himself trying to jam his right foot through the floor again.

"Listen, princess—"

"This is my car. My country. I know how fast I must go. And I would prefer it if you would not address me that way."

"As princess?" Nick frowned at her. "It's what you are, isn't it?"

"Not really. The Italian monarchy ceased to exist in 1946 so, to be accurate, titles have no meaning here anymore. They are a relic, a remnant, a—"

Beeeep! Beep beep beeeep!

"Merda," Nick shouted. "That car almost—"

"The driver is going too fast."

"He is not going too fast!" Nick hunkered down in his seat

and folded his arms over his chest. "I'd love to meet whoever taught you to drive," he muttered.

Alessia glanced at him, then back at the road.

Perhaps that was the problem, she thought nervously.

No one had taught her to drive. Not the way he meant. Of course, she wasn't going to tell him that. He was angry enough already, though why he should be was beyond her. She was driving carefully. Safely. It was how she always drove. Was it her fault that Italian drivers treated speed as a national pastime?

Besides, the truth about how she had learned to drive was too humiliating. No one need know she had only accomplished that feat a couple of years ago, that until then, her father's wishes had ruled her life.

This tough American gangster could not possibly understand what it was like to grow up the child of a father more interested in his own pleasures than in his family.

At sixteen, when she had asked to take driving lessons, her father had said driving a car was inappropriate for her status. At eighteen, away at a demure college in Rome, there had been no reason to learn to drive, not when public transportation was readily available. Besides, it was easier not to argue.

At twenty, she received her useless degree and took the slip of paper with her on a visit to her mother at the *sanatorio*. Her mother was having one of her lucid days. She looked at the heavily engraved bit of nonsense, looked at Alessia and said, "Do something with your life, *mia bambina*. Do not let him crush the spirit within you."

There was no question who that "him" was.

It was an epiphany. Alessia had returned home, packed, moved out. She took an apartment in Rome with three other girls. Her father was furious. How dare she disobey him?

He cut off her allowance.

She went to work as a waitress. It was all her expensive

education had prepared her for, aside from marrying a rich man, which was, naturally, what her father had hoped she would do.

One morning, she awoke thinking that it was pitiful to be living on her own and still not know how to drive. So she convinced one of her flatmates who owned an ancient Fiat to take her outside the city and let her get behind the wheel.

It had been a harrowing day—her friend had babbled prayers throughout—but when it was over, Alessia could drive. More or less. She'd managed to pass her licensing exam but she'd never learned to enjoy driving or to feel comfortable in heavy traffic.

And having a stranger seated beside her didn't help, especially when that stranger was Nicolo Orsini.

How could one man seem to fill the car with his presence, his irritation, his masculinity?

If only she had taken her father's car and driver to the airport to meet Orsini. Her father had urged her to, which was precisely why she had not done it. It was her own fault that she was trapped in what had suddenly become a too-small vehicle on a too-busy road with a too-macho male breathing fire beside her…

"Figlio di puttana!"

Nicolo Orsini's cry was almost as loud as the blast from the horn of a huge truck in the next lane. How had the Mercedes drifted so close to it? Alessia gave a shrill shriek; Nicolo leaned in, slapped his hands over hers and steered the car back into the proper lane. She knew the entire incident could not have taken more than a second to play out but in that second, she saw her life flash before her.

"That's it," the American roared. "Pull onto the shoulder."

Yes, she thought, yes, pull over, pull over, pull—

Nick wrested full control of the Mercedes from her. They

veered into the right-hand lane, then bounced onto the narrow shoulder, accompanied by a frenzied chorus of horns.

"The brake," he yelled, and, thank God, she responded. The car shuddered to a stop and he shut off the engine.

For a heartbeat, neither of them moved. Then Nick let go of the steering wheel. Alessia's hands dropped into her lap. Silence settled over the vehicle, broken only by the *tick tick tick* of the cooling engine.

Nick could feel his pulse tick-tick-ticking, too. He waited, fought for composure. Still, when he finally spoke, his voice was a hoarse croak.

"Get out of the car, Alessia."

She looked at him. "I beg your—"

"Do as I say! Get out of the damned car!"

Do as he said? She bristled. "I do not take orders from anyone!"

Nick let fly with a string of Sicilian obscenities he hadn't used or even thought of since he was a kid. He flung open his door, stalked around the automobile, yanked open her door, all but tore open her seat belt and physically lifted her from the car.

"What do you think you are doing?" Her voice rose; she wiggled like an eel, struck out at him with tightly balled fists. "Damn you, Nicolo Orsini! You have no right—"

"You almost got us killed."

"I did nothing of the sort. That truck driver—"

"The truck driver is probably heading for a place where he can change his underwear."

"You are not only rude, you are crude!"

"At least I'm not a danger to every poor soul who gets within a hundred miles of me!"

Alessia wanted to weep. He was right. She was terrified, horrified, appalled by what had almost happened but why would she admit that to such a man as this?

"Let go of me," she said sharply.

"Try that imperious tone on someone you haven't tried to kill. Now, get into the passenger seat and behave yourself!"

"I do not take orders! I am not…Mr. Orsini! *Signore!*" Alessia's voice climbed as Nick lifted her off her feet and slung her over his shoulder. Tears of rage rose in her eyes; she knotted her hands into fists and beat at his shoulders and back as he strode around the car. "You cannot do this!"

"Watch me," he said grimly, depositing her on her feet and reaching for the door.

"*Bastardo,*" she hissed. "*Siete come tutti i uomini!* You are the same as all men! You think women are incapable of taking care of themselves, that they need men to think for them—"

Enough, Nick thought, and he hauled Alessia to her toes and kissed her.

She gasped. Struggled. Fought him.

He went on kissing her.

And wondered, with almost clinical interest, why he was doing it.

Kissing her made no sense. A man kissed a woman because he liked her. Wanted her. Desired her and, God knew, he didn't like or want or desire the slippery-as-an-eel creature in his arms. Was he kissing her because he was angry? Hell, no. He had never kissed a woman out of anger. He didn't understand why a man would. Kissing wasn't about rage, it was about taste and texture.…

And then Alessia stopped struggling and he stopped thinking and the kiss turned into something hot and raw and primitive, and she went up on her toes and thrust her hands into his hair and he groaned, slid his hands under her jacket, under her blouse, felt the silky warmth of her skin and she said something against his mouth and he slid the tip of his tongue between her lips and…

A horn bleated.

A male voice yelled something into the night. Nick didn't understand the words, his Italian wasn't good enough for that, but he didn't have to be a linguist to figure it out.

His hands clasped her shoulders.

He lifted his head.

A shudder went through him.

He was standing by the side of a busy road holding a woman he didn't know and didn't like in his arms, maybe a heartbeat away from shoving her against the side of the car, pushing up her skirt, tearing off her panties and burying himself inside her.

Holy hell, he thought, and Alessia opened her eyes and stared at him, her expression blank.

"Easy," he said, and knew as soon as he said it that the word was inadequate.

The blank look on her face gave way to shock and then horror. She said something under her breath. His Italian wasn't good enough for him to understand that, either, but once again, he got the gist.

"I know," he said. "I'm sorry. I don't know what—"

She slapped him. Hard. His head jerked back at the force of the blow.

"Okay," he said, "if that made you feel bet—"

She slapped him again, or she would have, but he saw it coming and wrapped his hand around her wrist.

"That's enough," he said in a warning voice.

"You—you bastard! You pig! You—you brute!"

As obscenities went, he'd heard far worse. But that wasn't the point. He'd initiated the kiss, yes, but she'd been into it, all the way.

"Calm down, princess."

"Calm down? After what you did?"

Nick narrowed his eyes. "What I did," he said coldly, "was save us from being turned into roadkill."

"I am not talking about that. I am talking about that—that disgusting display of macho!" Eyes flashing, she jerked her hand free of his. "Who do you think you are?"

It was the most weary, clichéd line imaginable but it stung because he knew damned well what she meant by it. Nick moved closer, gratified to see her take a couple of quick steps back until she was pressed against the car.

"You know who I am, baby. I'm the man who's gonna save your daddy's royal ass, assuming you treat me right."

She recoiled. Hell, who could blame her? What kind of drivel was he spewing? And had a woman ever made him this angry before? He wanted to grab her and shake her.

Or grab her and kiss her again and again and again until she forgot who she was and who she was convinced he was, until she dragged his face down to hers and kissed him and kissed him…

Nick thought twice, stepped back, cleared his throat.

"Get in the car."

He could see her considering things. What in hell was there to consider? She couldn't drive worth a damn.

"Did you hear me, princess? Get in the car."

She stared up at him. What now? Her eyes were blurry with angry tears. As he'd already noted, her obviously expensive outfit was a mess. And somewhere along the way, maybe when he'd thrown her over his shoulder, she'd lost a shoe.

Still, she was beautiful.

Beautiful and vulnerable, and why he should notice or care was beyond him to comprehend.

He jerked his head toward the open passenger door. She lifted her chin in defiant acquiescence, in a way that made him want to laugh. He didn't; he wasn't that much of a fool. Instead, he slammed the door after her, went around the car—and yeah, there was her shoe, lying in the grass. He picked it up, tossed it in the backseat where it joined his carry-on bag and got behind the wheel.

Seconds later, they were on the highway, this time as part of the traffic flow.

They said nothing for the next hour. Then Alessia spoke.

"The sign for the vineyard is just ahead. You will turn to the right."

The headlights picked out a small wooden plaque. It said Antoninni in gilt letters; below it was a coat of arms. A griffin or maybe a lion, a shield and a sword. Nick's mouth twisted. What would the Orsini coat of arms be? A pistol, a dagger and a stack of money?

The turn opened onto a long, straight driveway, if you could call a half-mile-long road lined by poplars a driveway. Nick could see a shape on a rise ahead. It was a villa, big, imposing and graceful.

"You may park in front."

"How nice of you to say so."

Hell, he thought, what was that all about? She'd simply told him what he needed to know. Whose fault was it if the words sounded like a command?

He pulled in front of a set of wide marble steps. By the time he stepped from the car, Alessia was halfway up those steps, limping because she was wearing only the one shoe. Nick reached in back, collected his carry-on bag and the other shoe, then trotted up the stairs. Massive double doors opened, revealing bright light and a guy dressed like something out of a period movie.

"This is Joseph," Alessia said coolly. "He will show you to your rooms."

She tossed the words over her shoulder, the royal once again addressing the peasant. Nick smiled thinly.

"Princess?"

She turned and looked down her nose at him. Still smiling, he tossed her the shoe.

"You wouldn't want to go around half-naked," he said. "I mean, that was okay while you and I were alone, but—"

Her face filled with color. She opened her mouth, then snapped it shut, spun away from him and vanished down a long hallway. Joseph, to his credit, showed no change in expression.

"This way, please, *signore*," he said, reaching for Nick's bag.

"I'll carry my own bag, thanks."

A stupid, petty victory but a victory, nonetheless.

They climbed a long marble staircase to the second floor. The place was like a museum. High ceilings. Gilded cherubs. Paintings of shifty-eyed, long-faced ancestors peering from the walls.

Not a museum, Nick thought grimly. Museums had more warmth than this.

Joseph led him to a suite. Sitting room, bedroom, bathroom. Did the *signore* wish to have his bag unpacked? Nick said he didn't. Did he want something to eat? Nick almost said he didn't, strictly out of perversity, but then common sense took over and he said yes, a sandwich and some coffee would be fine.

Joseph bowed his way out. Nick closed the door, peeled off his suit jacket, his tie, undid a couple of buttons on his shirt, rolled up his sleeves and fell back on the bed, which was about half the size of a banquet hall. He folded his arms beneath his head and stared up at the ceiling, where it was vaguely possible a shepherd and shepherdess were about to do something they shouldn't.

The villa was obviously very, very old. And very, very expensive. Was he supposed to be impressed? His triplex in

New York was probably just as big and even if it wasn't filled with antiques, even if it had been built within the last twenty or so years, it was probably equal the cost to this, given the price of Manhattan real estate.

Nick snorted.

What was the matter with him?

He didn't give a damn about things like that.

He'd spent weekends at palatial estates in the Hamptons, others at one-room cabins in the Adirondacks, and he'd never thought of one as better than the other.

He sat up, unbuttoned his shirt, tossed it over the back of a chair and headed for the bathroom. What he needed was a long, hot shower, that sandwich and then a night's sleep.

Wrong.

The shower felt great. The butler delivered a well-laden tray, not only a sandwich and coffee, but also a small salad, some cheese, fruit and crackers. The bed was comfortable. But at 2:00 a.m., Nick was still awake, standing outside on the small Juliet balcony despite the chill in the night air, staring out at a moonlit garden.

Something had awakened him....

There. A figure. A woman, wearing something long and filmy, her hair a pale spill of gold down her back, walking slowly along one of the garden paths.

Alessia.

Nick didn't think. He pulled on a pair of jeans. Shirtless, barefoot, he let himself out of his suite, went down the stairs, through the silent house to a back door and stepped out into the garden and the night. He reached her in seconds, cupped her shoulders and turned her toward him. She looked surprised but not afraid. If anything, she looked—she looked—

"*Signore.*"

"My name is Nick," he said, his voice low.

God, she was beautiful. Exquisite. A fairy-tale princess come to life.

She hesitated. *Say my name,* he thought, as if it were a battle to be won. After a second's hesitation, she took a deep breath.

"Nicolo. What are you doing out here?"

"I couldn't sleep. Obviously, neither could you."

"*Sì.* I—I keep thinking about what happened before. On the road."

"Yeah. So do I."

"*È colpa mia,*" she whispered. "It was my fault. I—I do not drive very well."

Another time, he would have laughed. It was the understatement of the year.

"No. You don't." He reached out, tucked a strand of gold behind her ear. "But I wasn't talking about your driving." He cupped her face in his hands, lifted it to his. "I'm talking about that kiss."

Even in the moonlight, he could see the delicate rise of color in her face.

"I do not wish to discuss it."

No. Why would she? She didn't like what he was. He didn't like what she was. It was not an auspicious start for anything, not even a business deal.

And she was right. He didn't want to discuss it, either. Instead, he drew her into his arms, kissed her more and more deeply until she was clinging to him.

Then he let go of her, turned his back and walked away.

CHAPTER FIVE

NICK was an early riser.

You had to be, in the Marine Corps, and the habit stuck even after he'd returned to civilian life, though by now it was more a preference than a habit. There was something restful about early morning silence, especially in Manhattan; a run through Central Park before it was flooded with tourists, before the surrounding streets were jammed with traffic…

Unless, of course, there was a woman in his bed.

Wake-up sex was one of life's absolute pleasures.

But there was no woman in his bed today, no Central Park just across the street. What he woke to were thoughts of a woman and, dammit, those thoughts had kept him awake half the night.

Who was Alessia Antoninni? Maybe the better question was, what was she? A princess—hell, an Ice Princess. And why should it matter? He didn't like her, he resented the class system to which she belonged and there was no doubt that she felt exactly the same way about him. Heaven knew he didn't have to love a woman to want her—if such a thing as love even existed—but he sure as hell had to like her.

The situation didn't make sense—and as dawn painted the sky with streaks of crimson and pink, Nick gave up all pretence at sleep, flung back the covers, tugged on an old corps

T-shirt, shorts and sneakers, made his way down the balcony steps and took off on a run he badly needed.

Five miles. Seven. Eight. He had no idea how far he went, only that he couldn't find a way to get all his questions about the Ice Princess out of his head even as sweat blurred his vision and his lungs began to labor.

The sun was climbing the sky by the time he returned to the villa. He ran inside, up the staircase and to his suite, went straight to the bathroom, turned on the water in the sink and scooped some into his hands.

The good news was that the water was wet. The bad was that it was warm. What he wanted was a long, cool drink. Surely there'd be bottled water in the kitchen.

It was definitely worth a try.

Nick blotted his face and shoulders with a towel, draped it around his neck, shoved his dark hair back from his forehead, then opened the door that led to the hall.

The place was still quiet.

Okay, then.

He went down the stairs and headed toward the rear of the house, where he guessed the kitchen would be.

Excellent.

There wasn't anyone in sight, not a cook or a maid or the butler. The big room was empty....

Except, it wasn't.

Alessia was there, standing in front of the open refrigerator, head tilted back as she drank from a bottle of water.

The sight startled him. He came to a fast stop and the sole of one sneaker caught on the tile floor. The resultant squeak was as shrill as the cry of a nighthawk.

She spun toward him. The bottle slipped in her hand; she caught it but not before some of the water had splashed down her chin, her throat and onto her cotton tank top. Nick watched the water darken the fabric over one breast.

His belly knotted. Stupid, he thought, to react to the sight of a wet tank top.

"What are you doing here?"

She sounded as if she'd discovered him with his hands buried in a wall safe. Obviously, she hadn't expected him to walk in on her, or to see yesterday's cool, if rumpled, business-woman replaced by a woman in shorts, tank and sneakers, blond hair pulled into a ponytail, face and body damp with sweat.

And one breast—one high, rounded breast—tantalizingly darkened by that splash of water.

Without warning, he remembered how she had looked last night in the garden, her hair loose on her shoulders, her nightgown filmy and feminine in the moon's soft glow—and thought, too, of how he had kissed her, how she had kissed him back....

Nick raised his gaze to her face. Her color was high; he could see her pulse beating fast in the hollow of her throat. Was she thinking about that kiss, too?

"*Signore*. What are you doing here?"

So much for remembering last night. Nick flashed a tight smile. "Stealing the family silver."

"I didn't mean..." Her color deepened. "You startled me, that's all."

"Yeah. Sorry." He shrugged. "I was out running. I came back and wanted something cold to drink." His eyes swept over her again. "You were running, too."

Alessia swallowed hard. It was a statement, not a question, and it made no sense that it should bother her. So what if Nicolo Orsini knew she'd been out running? She ran every morning no matter where she was; she had discovered the freedom of it years ago, even before she'd left here forever, the sense that if you ran fast enough, hard enough, you could leave your old self behind.

You couldn't, of course. She knew that now. Still, she ran. She loved the burn of muscle, the rise of sweat. Her father thought it was unladylike and perhaps that was part of what made it so appealing....

Why was Nicolo Orsini looking at her that way? His dark eyes moved over her like a slow caress, lingering on her mouth, her throat.

Her body.

He made her feel as if too much of her was exposed. Not physically; she wore less than this at the beach. It was something more complicated, a realization that he was seeing a side of her that was not his business to see.

It made her recall last night. How he had kissed her, how she had kissed him back.

To her horror, she felt her nipple pebble under her water-stained tank top, her flesh lift as if in anticipation of his touch. Instinct told her to turn and run. Logic told her running would be the most dangerous thing she could do.

Instead, she lifted her chin.

"This is my home," she said coolly. "If I wish to run here, I am free to do so."

Dio, how stupid she sounded! Why did her words, her thoughts, get all twisted when she spoke to this man?

His eyes narrowed. He folded his arms over his chest. It was an impressive chest, tanned and muscled as were his arms.

"Sure." His voice was toneless. "I should have asked permission."

"No," she said quickly, "no, of course not. I only meant..." She had no idea what she'd meant, she thought unhappily. She was talking at the speed of a runaway train and making about as much sense. Quickly, she turned toward the fridge, took out a bottle of water and held it toward him. "You must be thirsty."

That won her a small smile. "Thanks."

Their fingers brushed as he took the bottle from her. A tiny electric jolt went through her. She gave a nervous laugh.

"Static electricity," she said.

"Electricity, for sure," Nick said, his eyes on hers. Then he unscrewed the bottle top, tilted his head back and took a long, deep drink. A tiny trickle of water trailed over his bottom lip, traced a path down his long, tanned throat.

The water would taste salty there, right there, if she touched her tongue to it....

She made a little sound, turned it into a cough, but it didn't help keep her knees from feeling weak.

Nicolo lowered the bottle of water, looked at her with one dark eyebrow lifted.

Say something, Alessia told herself fiercely, something clever.

She couldn't. She was tongue-tied. She, who made her living chatting up clients, being the intermediary between often hostile groups, was at a complete loss for words.

But her brain was working overtime.

Dio, this man was beautiful! She didn't like him, would never like him, but you didn't have to like a man to admit he was, in a word, *spectacular.*

Such broad shoulders. Such well-defined muscles. His shirt was wet, stuck to his skin, delineating cut abs and a flat belly that led to narrow hips and long, muscular legs. And his face. The face of an angel. Or a devil. Strong. Masculine. A hard mouth that could take hers with dark passion or soft tenderness...

"...just you and me. Together."

Alessia blinked. He was watching her, eyes narrowed to obsidian slits under thick, sooty lashes. She felt her face heat.

"Just you and me, what?"

Those dark eyebrows rose again.

"Run, of course. What else could I have possibly meant?"

"No. I don't think so. I mean—I mean…" Dammit, what *did* she mean? She swung away from him, placed her empty water bottle on the countertop beside the sink. "We'd better get started," she said briskly. "We meet with my father's people in an hour."

She swept past him, head high, spine straight, every inch the princess though he knew damned well that she'd been something else for a little while. He'd had women look at him that way before; he knew what it meant.

What he'd never before experienced was such a swift, gut-churning reaction.

That was the reason he'd deliberately lightened the atmosphere with a pathetic quip. If he hadn't—hell, if he hadn't, he'd have done what he wanted, what he damned well knew they both wanted, right here.

Grab her wrist. Swing her toward him. Capture her in his arms, cover her mouth with his. Breathe in the sweaty, earthy, real-woman scent that rose from her skin. Lift her onto the countertop, put his mouth to her throat, her nipples, suck them deep into his mouth right through her wet shirt while he put his hand between her thighs, slipped his fingers under the edge of her shorts, felt her heat, her wetness because she would be hot and wet and eager, eager for his possession…

Nick shuddered.

He watched Alessia walk down the hall, watched her until she vanished from sight. Then he drank the last of the water in one long swallow, went back to his rooms and took the longest, coldest shower of his life.

It didn't help.

Ten minutes later, getting out of the shower, he was still thinking about her and what had happened—what had *not* happened—in the kitchen.

Thinking that way was, to put it bluntly, ridiculous.

So, okay. He wouldn't think about her. Not anymore.

He toweled off, dressed in what he thought of as his invest-ment banker uniform. Custom-made white broadcloth shirt. Deep red Hermès tie. Gold cuff links. Black wing tips. Dark gray Armani suit. Hey, one Armani deserved another, and she would surely wear her best today.

Well, so would he. The reflection that looked back at him from the mirrored dressing room wall was businesslike. Professional. The Ice Princess would still see him as a grown-up punk, but—

But, he was back to square one, wasting time thinking about her.

Thinking about the effect she had on him.

Even if he could get past the I-Am-To-The-Manor-Born and You-Are-A-Peasant crap, the lady wasn't his type. Attractive? Sure. But he couldn't imagine her trying to please a man, ever. Not just him but any man. And yes, he liked an accommodat-ing woman, and if it was sexist, who cared?

Nick frowned, stared in the mirror, shot his cuffs, smoothed down his tie.

The only way to explain his attraction to her, if you could call it that, would be if he were horny. He wasn't. He had a healthy appetite for sex but he'd just been with a woman, what, the day before yesterday? And even if he hadn't, he'd never been the kind of man who'd jump the bones of any female just because she was there.

Besides, Alessia wasn't there, not in the real sense of the word. She'd made it clear he wasn't her type any more than she was his.

His frown became a scowl.

Then, how come she'd responded when he'd kissed her? And, yes, she had responded. A woman didn't moan into a man's mouth, didn't wind her arms around his neck, didn't press her body against his unless she was feeling something.

Hell.

A hard-on was not the right accessory for an Armani suit.

Okay. This was nonsense.

Nick drew a long, deep breath.

He was a logical man but even he had to admit that were times logic just didn't work, and this was one of those times. So, back to plan A. Yes, he'd invest in the vineyard, not for Cesare but for himself, if only because backing out of that decision now could be interpreted as weakness.

But two days was all he'd spend here. Forget what he'd told her yesterday, that he'd need two weeks.

Two days was, exactly as he'd originally intended, more than enough time to go over the vineyard's financial records. Meet with the prince's people. Eyeball the operation. Appoint an administrator to oversee things. Then he'd be on the first plane for New York—if it was quicker, he'd have the Orsini jet fly over to get him.

And if that seemed like the cowardly way out, it wasn't.

It was a businesslike approach, and business was what this was all about.

She was waiting for him at the foot of the stairs.

Yesterday's ice maiden was back, this time unrumpled.

Neat chignon, or whatever women called that bun they made at the back of their heads. White silk blouse. Black pumps. Gray Armani suit. He almost laughed. They were almost identical, if you omitted the lush rise of her breasts and the long, long legs beneath her slender skirt.

Her eyes swept over him, her look an appraising one. Nick offered a thin smile.

"It's the latest in gangster-wear in New York."

If he'd thought to embarrass her, he'd failed.

"And so much more attractive than tattoos that say 'Mother,'" she said sweetly.

"Why, princess. You've practically seen me naked. You know damned well I don't have any tattoos."

Color flooded her face.

"I have not seen you naked," she said, her voice gone cold.

Nick shrugged. "Close enough."

"And never any closer, I assure you."

He took a step toward her. To his gratification, she took a step back.

"A challenge, princess?" he said, very softly.

"A statement of fact, Mister Orsini."

He gave her a slow smile. There was something about her when she was like this, just the slightest bit off balance, that was very appealing.

"A challenge," he said again.

And then, because it seemed the only thing to do, he bent his head and brushed his mouth lightly over hers.

Her lips were soft. Warm. Did they tremble just a little under the light pressure of his? There was only one way to find out. Nick cupped her face in one hand and kissed her again, a longer kiss this time, his lips slightly parted as they covered hers and, yes, her mouth was trembling, her breathing was quick, she was rising on her toes, leaning toward him and now her lips parted, too...

She made a sound, put her hands against his chest and her eyes flew open and fixed on his. He saw endless questions in their deep blue depths, questions he suspected were identical to his. For a heartbeat, he thought of answering them all, for her and for him, by taking her in his arms and kissing her until she begged him to finish this insane thing between them.

Maybe it wasn't what was happening that was crazy.

Maybe it was him.

"Alessia."

His voice was rough as sandpaper. He took her hands in his, sought desperately for something clever to say, but nothing came. Her eyes were blurred, her breathing uneven, and he knew his wasn't any too steady.

"Nicolo," she said in shaky whisper.

It was the second time she'd said his name. How come he was so aware of that, and aware, too, that it sounded different, in her mouth? What she said was "Neekello," and how could a simple word sound like pure sex?

Nick let go of her while he still could and put a few inches of space between them. She swayed; he reached out, steadied her with a hand on her elbow. She drew a deep breath, sank her very white teeth into the rich curve of her bottom lip.

The simple action damned near undid him.

"This—this must stop," she whispered. "This—this thing between us…"

Her words drifted to silence. A muscle jumped in his jaw.

He knew that any other woman in this kind of situation would have laid the blame strictly on the guy. It made him want to kiss her again but he wouldn't. Dammit, he wouldn't. He wouldn't so much as touch her again, and absolutely, positively he was saying, *arrivederci,* ASAP tomorrow.

"You're right," he said briskly. "It has to stop. In fact, it just did. Let's go to that meeting you've set up, come back here and check out the vineyards, the winery, all of it, so I can be out of here tomorrow."

"But you said—"

"I know what I said." God, he wanted to touch her. Just one quick brush of his hands over her body… "I've changed my mind. In fact, I'll put a call in, arrange for the Orsini plane to fly over and get me. It'll be quicker that way."

"The Orsini plane."

"Yes. We have our own—"

"Of course you do," Alessia said, and all at once, her eyes were clear and cool. "For a moment, I almost forgot who you were, *signore*. *Molte grazie* for reminding me."

The temperature dropped ten degrees. If she'd slapped him across the face, she couldn't have made things any clearer.

The time was right to tell her who he was. What he was. That he and his old man had nothing but blood in common... And then he thought, to hell with that. To hell with explaining himself to Alessia Antoninni or anyone else.

"I understand, *principessa*." His tone was as frigid as hers. "Lust can get in the way of sanity."

Her cheeks flamed. She called him something he couldn't quite understand and he thought of returning the compliment but, dammit, no way was he going to let her turn him into the kind of man she believed him to be.

"Undoubtedly," he said, his smile feral. Then he gestured toward the front door. "After you, baby."

Back straight as an arrow, she spun on her heel and marched to the door. She didn't wait for him to play the gentleman; she flung it open herself and marched down the marble steps, straight toward a black Bentley the size of a not-so-small boat. A liveried chauffeur shot from the driver's seat, opened the rear door and bowed as she stepped past him into the car.

Nick followed after her. "Do not," he growled to the chauffeur, "do not even *think* of bowing to me!"

Aside from that, he was more than willing to let somebody else do the driving.

Somebody whose head was on straight, he thought grimly, as the car started majestically down the long driveway.

CHAPTER SIX

ALESSIA had arranged for the meeting to be held in the offices her father kept in Florence.

The building itself had once been a palace and was very old, dating back to the 1400s and the Renaissance, when the Medici family ruled the city.

The Antoninnis could trace their lineage to Cosimo de' Medici or, rather, to a supposedly illegitimate son of Cosimo's. Faced with his mistress's threats to make their affair a public scandal, Cosimo was said to have given her the vast, fertile rolling acres that even then were producing excellent wine. When the illegitimate son died, as so many Medicis, legitimate or not, were wont to do at that time, the mistress passed the estate on to her daughter, who married a prince of the house of Antoninni, which was when the vineyards became known by that name.

The Antoninni part of the tale was true; there was some doubt about the Medici connection but no Antoninni had ever tried to verify it. Someone in each generation always realized that tracing something that might turn out to be a centuries-old falsehood—or, worse still, a tale of murder—would serve no purpose except to disgrace the Antoninni–Medici connection.

Alessia thought the whole thing was foolish. Who had the time for titles and lineage and fifteenth-century intrigue?

Besides, the Antoninni problem right now was not one of DNA but of dollars. Orsini dollars, ones that would become Antoninni euros. That was the reason she had arranged to hold the meeting here, in these magnificent surroundings.

"An excellent plan," her father had said, assuming that she meant to impress their foreign guest.

Alessia's motives had been far less admirable.

In terms of power and wealth, Nicolo Orsini was the modern version of Cosimo de' Medici, but with one enormous difference.

Cosimo had been a man of refinement and honor.

Nicolo was not.

And if her motives for bringing him here took her down to his level, so be it.

She had no choice but to deal with him. She did have a choice as to the way in which she did it, and impressing him was not on her agenda.

What she wanted was to remind him of where he existed on the social scale, that he no more belonged in this beautiful city, this jewel of a palace, than a junkyard dog belonged in a roomful of poodles.

In other words, she wanted him to be ill at ease.

Yes, she admitted, glancing at him as the big car glided to a stop before the palazzo, it was petty. She'd permitted herself a moment of guilt but only a moment because of the satisfaction it promised. Nicolo Orsini might have a polished look to him, he might speak passable Italian, even if it was tainted by the rough dialect of Sicily. He might have all the manners, all the money in the world, but he was not a gentleman.

He wasn't even an honest businessman.

He was a bandit all gussied up in fancy clothes, and she'd known that before she ever set eyes on him. Now that she had, now that she'd seen, firsthand, how he took what he wanted, how he…he thought nothing of forcing himself on a woman who clearly wanted nothing to do with him…

He had kissed her.

Her cheeks flushed.

And…and if she had seemed to let it happen, even to participate, it was only because she was—she was—

Dio, what was she?

Why had she permitted a man like this to put his mouth on hers? Why had she spent part of the night imagining how that mouth, that hot, firm mouth would feel on her breasts?

"Principessa?"

Alessia blinked. The chauffeur stood at rigid attention beside the open passenger door of the Bentley.

She took a deep breath. "Oh. *Sì,* Guillermo. *Grazie.*"

The man dipped his head, a gesture she despised but this was no time to remind him of it, not when Nicolo had moved across the seat, not when she could feel the heated pressure of his thigh against hers.

She stepped quickly from the car; he followed after her.

"We will be ready to return to the villa in two hours," she told the chauffeur, who did that damned lowering-of-the-head thing again. "And do not do that," she said irritably. She heard Nicolo snort and she swung toward him. "Do you see something amusing?"

"Not amusing," he said lazily. "Perplexing. The man is treating you as you wish to be treated. And you fault him for it?"

"I have not asked him to bow to me!"

"You don't have to. Every breath you take makes it clear that you are part of the aristocracy."

She felt her face turn pink. "You know nothing about me, *signore,* and yet you feel free to judge me?"

The faint smile on his lips faded. "There's an American

expression, Alessia. 'Right back at you.' If you don't know what it means, I'll be happy to explain."

Dio, the impertinence of the man. Alessia swallowed her irritation and marched through the tall golden gates that guarded the palace.

"Wow."

Wow. She almost laughed. Her unwelcome guest, her father's onerous hope of salvation, sounded as she'd expected him to sound, as if he were entering a Disney World building.

"This is quite a structure. Which Medici built it?"

She stopped and looked at him. He stood with his face turned up to the spectacular gold cherubs on the building's facade.

"I beg your pardon?"

"I know it's Medici. It has to be. But was this Giovanni's work? Cosimo's? Lorenzo's? Lorenzo, I'd bet. The others were benefactors of the city, too, but he was the one with the soul of an artist. Am I right?"

"You know of the Medicis?"

Nick looked at her. He could read the astonishment on her face.

"Yes," he said coolly. "I do. Surprised?"

"No. Not at all."

She was a beautiful liar. He was damned certain she'd expected him to assume this perfect little structure had been put up by Disney.

"And you are correct," she added briskly. "Lorenzo was its benefactor."

He nodded. "That figures."

"But Cosimo is one of our ancestors."

Had she really said that? Judging by the lift of his eyebrows, she had. It was not an appreciative lift, either; he saw the boast just as much a foolish one as she did. Still, boasting, if more subtly than that, was the reason she'd brought her father's crime-boss investor to this place.

She would have to keep one thought ahead of him at all times.

A golden cage of an elevator, installed in the mid-1800s, whisked them to the third floor. The meeting room, the one she had carefully chosen, was directly opposite. It was the most glorious chamber of all the glorious chambers in the small, elegant palace.

"After you," the man she was trying to intimidate said politely, and she led him inside.

There was no "wow" this time but she could hear the intake of his breath as he took in the surroundings: the marble-topped table, the gilded vases filled with flowers, the thick silk carpet that was almost as old as the building itself, the Michelangelos and Raphaels and Donatellos hanging on the walls.

Orsini was impressed. And, she was certain, most assuredly aware that he was out of place. The thought gave her another guilty twinge but she dismissed it.

She might have to eat her pride by ferrying this man around as if he were not who he was, but it would surely be worth it.

The five men seated at the marble-topped table rose to greet him. Oh, yes, he was in over his head today. Her father's attorney. Her father's accountant. The vineyard manager. The viniculturist and the vintner.

Alessia watched Nicolo shake hands with each of them.

Then she sat back, ready to watch him eat crow. An American expression, and an excellent one.

What could a gangster possibly know of the law, of finance or of *vino?*

Five minutes later, she knew she had made a terrible error in judgment.

"Ah," he told the attorney, "what a pleasure to meet the man who won Palmieri versus Shott in Venice last year." Alessia watched the lawyer sit up straighter.

"You know of that case, *signore?*" he said, and Orsini replied that yes, of course he did, it had made headlines everywhere.

The accountant turned brick-red with delight when Nicolo said he was delighted to meet the man responsible for such an outstanding article in a prior month's international finance journal.

He made no pretence at knowing anything at all about wine.

"Except how to enjoy a good vintage," he said, which made everyone laugh, even the vintner and viniculturist, who were the worst wine snobs imaginable.

Finally, he looked around the room and took long looks at the paintings her father had not sold only because he had understood there was more to gain from being known as a man who owned such things than from giving them up.

"Magnificent," he said, and added, casually, that he'd been fortunate enough to have acquired a Donatello at Sotheby's a few months ago and had his agent keeping an eye out for a Raphael rumored to be coming on the market soon.

By the time they got down to business, her father's people were eating out of his hand.

But that changed. Once the niceties were out of the way, Orsini the gentleman gave way to Orsini the thug....

Alessia gave an imperceptible shake of her head.

No. Not fair. He wasn't a thug. Not today, anyway. Seated across from her was a sophisticated, powerful, blunt man who was as smart as anyone in the room. Smarter, she suspected. He understood finances.

And that he was being lied to.

He'd listened without expression as the accountant and the attorney danced around the questions he had asked. Why did a successful vineyard suddenly stop earning a profit? Why was it failing? More to the point, what would it take to make the place a success again?

The answers were interesting. He seemed to think so, too....

Until, after twenty or thirty minutes, he held up his hand and said, "Enough."

This was, he said, pure fiction. Nicely done fiction, but fiction nevertheless. Then he pushed aside the documents spread over the table. His obsidian eyes were as merciless as those of a marauding shark.

"Assuming I decide to put money into this operation, it will be because I see a good reason to do so."

"But we understood..." The attorney looked beseechingly at the accountant. "We understood it was your father who would make the loan to the prince."

"I will be the one making it," Nick said brusquely. "And none of what I've seen or heard makes me eager to turn over ten million euros."

"Ten mill—"

"Ten million, that's right." He looked from one man to the other, then at Alessia. "The terms of the loan have also changed. I will expect to own a fifty-one percent interest in Antoninni Vineyards."

"No," Alessia said quickly. "We are not selling our vineyard to you."

"It's your father's vineyard, and he will do whatever I ask or there will be no loan." Nick turned to the attorney and accountant. "My own people will want to see these documents. As for the condition of the vines and land..." He looked at the other men. "Can they be saved if money is diverted to them, or have they been allowed to deteriorate for too long?"

"They most assuredly can be saved," the viniculturist

said eagerly, as the vintner and property manager nodded in agreement.

"Excellent." Nick rose to his feet, motioned those three to remain seated and nodded at the attorney and accountant. "In that case, gentlemen, I'll expect the legal and financial data to be faxed to my New York office by the end of the week."

The attorney opened his mouth to protest, then thought better of it. So did the accountant. It was clear they had been dismissed as if they were errant schoolboys.

Alessia snorted. She tried to turn the sound into a cough but Nicolo's raised eyebrows said he knew the difference between the two.

"Is there something you wanted to say, princess?"

"Only what I have already said. My father will not agree to giving you controlling interest in what has been a family-owned property for many centuries."

She saw his mouth thin. Then he drew back her chair and smiled pleasantly to the three remaining men.

"The princess and I will be just a moment. Alessia? Let's step into the hall."

She didn't want to go with him. Foolish, she knew; there was no reason to avoid being alone with him and so she stood up and preceded him out the door. The attorney and accountant were gone; she could hear the faint buzz of conversation start up in the room behind her.

"You'd better accept this, princess, and so had your father," Nicolo Orsini said calmly. "I won't invest in the vineyard without an assurance that it can be made profitable, nor will I invest in it without owning a majority share."

"That's not going to happen. You knew about my father's financial woes before you came here. I know you did. And you never even suggested you'd demand ownership."

"I came here as my father's emissary. He didn't care how badly your father had screwed up, but I do."

"Because you changed the rules," Alessia said with indignation. "You decided to invest your own money, not your father's. Why did you do that?"

It was, Nick thought, a good question. He'd tried finding an answer before but he kept coming up empty. All he knew was that instinct told him there was more going on here than met the eye and that it somehow involved the woman glaring at him.

His life had been ruled by logic, but he had to admit, there were times a man could do better by relying on instinct. It was instinct that had kept him alive more than once in the hellholes in which he'd served his country, and while this surely wasn't a life-or-death situation, he had the sense that instinct was still the way to go.

"I changed my plans and decided to invest my own money because investing is what I do."

She laughed, and Nick narrowed his eyes. "I know you find that hard to believe, but that is exactly what I do."

"Right," she said sarcastically. "You invest in vineyards."

"In all kinds of properties, but not in ones that aren't worth my time or resources."

"Antoninni is very much worth your time and money!"

Her voice trembled; she'd been so caught up in watching him, watching how he dealt with her father's impressionable lackeys, that she'd almost forgotten what the stakes were.

Her mother's welfare.

That was what mattered, not her anger at having to deal with this man or the future of the vineyard. Mama was what counted, and what would happen to her if Nicolo didn't put millions into her father's hands. His unfettered hands, because the last thing her father would want would be Nicolo Orsini looking over his shoulder, telling him he could or could not spend ten million euros.

"Nicolo." She drew a deep breath, smiled in what she hoped

was a reassuring way. "Isn't it enough to invest in Tuscan property? There's no reason to own any. I mean, you are not Tuscan—"

She gasped as his fingers dug into her shoulders.

"No," he growled, "I'm American. Sicilian-American, and that puts me on a different plane, or so you think."

"No! I didn't mean—"

"I am an Orsini, Alessia, but that doesn't mean I am a fool."

"I did not suggest—"

"Never lie to me, princess. It's the one thing I won't ever forgive."

Her color rose; she could feel it in her face. "I am not a liar! I'm simply trying to figure out why you are so determined to take control of the vineyard from my father."

"Because that's the way I want it."

"But if he won't let you and if you walk away and don't give him the money—"

"What?" His eyes searched hers. "What is the real reason this is so important to you?"

Alessia stared at him. He was so powerful. So capable of holding the world in his hands, and never mind how he had earned that power. He was a man who could do anything; she had known that from the moment she first saw him.

What if she told him everything? About why she had agreed to deal with him. About her father's vicious threat. About her mother and how only he, Nicolo Orsini, a stranger from another world, one she detested, could save her.

"Tell me the truth, Alessia. I know there's more to this than you're letting me see."

His voice was low. His hands no longer bit into her shoulders, they cupped them instead. She looked up into his face, into his dark, deep eyes. She could tell him the truth....

And then what?

He was a ruthless thug. Forget his beautiful face and body. His manners. His ability to tell Donatello from Donald Duck. He was what he was, and she could never trust him.

"There's nothing more to this than you see, *signore*," she said coolly. "I'm just a good Tuscan daughter, determined to do all I can for my *papa*."

Nicolo's mouth twisted. He let go of her, walked back into the conference room with Alessia behind him.

"Gentlemen," he said, "tell me what I need to know."

The manager spoke in glowing terms of the land. The viniculturist talked excitedly of what he would do to improve the vines, given the money and the time. The vintner talked of past vintages, of future ones, of how he could return Antoninni Wines to their past glories.

Then there was silence. Even Alessia held her breath.

Nick smiled. "I'm impressed. Not just impressed, I'm pleased." He pushed back his chair and rose to his feet. So did the others, including Alessia. "If I go through with this deal, *signori,* I'll want you all to stay on."

Beaming smiles. Handshakes. The men trooped out of the room and Nick turned, folded his arms and leaned back against the table, the look in his eyes indecipherable.

"Okay," he said. "I'm waiting."

"For what?"

"For the rest of the sell."

"The rest of the…the presentation? That was all of it. Well, you will meet the mayor tonight and some others who live nearby, but—"

"Aren't you going to make a pitch, too?"

Her chin rose. His tone was insulting; they both knew it.

"The pitch, as you call it, was just made, *signore*."

"Really?" He unwound from where he stood. There was no other word to describe the lazy straightening of that long, muscular male body, or the slow way he came toward her.

"Because it occurs to me, princess, that you might be part of the sell."

"That I…?" Her head jerked up. "I have no idea what you mean."

But she did. He could see it in her eyes as he reached out and drew a slow finger down her face, down her throat, pausing just at the demure V-neck of her silk blouse.

"Those kisses. The little moans—"

"There have been no moans, little or otherwise," she snapped, slapping his hand away.

Nick said nothing. How come he hadn't thought of it sooner? The idea had come to him while the accountant and the attorney were doing their little dance, trying to convince him the prince wasn't as desperate for money as Nick already knew he was, thanks to what his father had told him and thanks, too, to some quiet checking he'd done on his own.

"But there have been kisses, princess. You won't deny that."

"Kisses you instigated."

"Kisses you responded to."

"Only because I did not expect them!"

He raised one dark eyebrow. "You always kiss a man back when he unexpectedly kisses you?"

"I did not mean that at all!"

No, he thought, he was pretty sure she hadn't meant that, pretty sure that the Ice Princess wouldn't return a man's kiss unless her hormones had taken over for her head.

She'd set this meeting here so she could remind him of who he was as compared to who she was. He was onto all that and it certainly didn't improve his attitude toward her.

So why, despite those things, did she melt when he kissed her? Hell, why did he react the same way, losing sight of everything except the urgent need to get her into bed?

None of it made sense…unless the touch me, don't touch

me routine was part of the scheme, part of making him crazy enough to go along with whatever she and her old man wanted.

He could kiss her again, right now, and try to unravel the mystery....

Instead, he took a quick step back.

"Okay," he said briskly. "Okay, if you don't have a second part to this presentation, I do."

She looked up at him. "I told you, there is a second part. Tonight's dinner."

"Is your closet only an adjunct to the local Armani shop?"

She blinked. *"Scusi?"*

"Do you own anything except those suits?"

Alessia looked down at herself, then back at him.

"Sì. Yes. But I don't under—"

"You grew up on those acres of grapes, didn't you?"

"Well, yes, of course, but—"

"I want a tour. With you as my guide, not the viniculturist or the vintner or anybody else. Put on jeans or whatever it is you wear when you're being a real person."

"I beg your pardon, *signore!* I *am* a real—"

"A real person," he said firmly, and he laughed at the indignant expression on her lovely face and then he stopped laughing and did exactly what he'd told himself he would not do—reached for her, gathered her against him, kissed her—and it took less than a second before she moaned, rose to him and parted her lips to his.

It wasn't enough.

Nick cursed, slid his hands under her skirt, bunched it at her thighs and felt her shudder. She whispered something in soft, frantic Italian and she wrapped her arms around him, dug her hands into his hair as he slid his hands down into her panties, cupped her bottom, brought her tightly against him and she moaned again at the feel of his erection—

A knock sounded at the door.

"Principessa?"

The chauffeur. Alessia shoved her hands against Nick's chest. He drew her even closer.

"Send him away."

"Principessa? You said two hours. I have told that to the *carabiniere* but he threatens me with *uno biglietto*."

"You're a princess," Nick whispered. "How can you get a parking ticket?"

Alessia gave a soft laugh. It made him smile. That he could make her laugh seemed almost as important as that he could make her melt in his arms.

"I understand, Guillermo," she said loudly. "Go down and wait for us, please. We'll be there in a moment."

"Alessia…"

She shook her head, pressed her hands lightly against Nick's chest and he gave in to the inevitable and let her step free of his embrace. She smoothed her hair, her jacket, her skirt. Then she opened the door and Nick followed her into the elevator. Just before the doors opened, he gave in to instinct, pulled her against him and gave her a hard, deep kiss.

"This isn't over," he said against her mouth.

"Yes," she said in a tone that didn't match the race of her heart against his, "it is. I shall see you tonight. Seven o'clock, in the—"

"You're taking me on a guided tour of the vineyard."

"Listen to me, Nicolo…"

"I am listening," he said roughly, "not to your words but to what you tell me when you kiss me." And when her lips parted in protest, he used it as a chance to kiss her one last time before he let her go.

CHAPTER SEVEN

BACK in the guest suite, Nick tried to get a handle on what in hell was happening.

He was in a baffling situation, one he didn't entirely control, and it made him angry.

Angry at the prince for creating a financial disaster that had opened the door to Cesare's intervention. At Cesare for dumping the problem on him. At Alessia, who behaved as if she were as confused by her reaction to him as he was by his reaction to her.

Or was she?

Maybe that second of insight he'd had during the meeting a little while ago was right on the money. Maybe she was playing a game as old as time and as dangerous as anything he'd ever faced, even in combat.

He tore off his jacket and the rest of his Wall Street attire because a man this enraged shouldn't be wearing the trappings of civilization.

Damn them all. His father. Her father. The Ice Princess.

"Hell," Nick swore, and, naked, he stalked into the bathroom, slapped his hands on the marble vanity and glared at his reflection in the mirror.

Why lie about it?

The person he was furious with was himself.

He was letting a woman make a fool of him.

Yes, he'd let his father use a despicable trick to get him to come here. If his mother really wanted a bit of Tuscany, why would Cesare have waited all these years to buy it for her? And why this place, this vineyard owned by a family whose roots were probably entwined not just with the Medicis but with the double-dealing and conspiracy of the Borgias?

Nick didn't give a damn. Not about Cesare's real motives or the prince screwing up an enterprise his family had owned for five hundred years. What mattered was that he was being used. By his old man, whose entire life was given over to conspiracy. By a prince who didn't know the meaning of honor.

And by a woman.

A woman who was manipulating him.

And he—dammit, he had allowed it to happen. He'd let her draw him deeper and deeper into a dark whirlpool of desire more intense than any he'd ever known.

There could only be two explanations for her behavior.

Either she was willing to do anything to make sure he invested in the vineyard.

Or she was taking a walk on the wild side.

Not that it mattered.

He'd had enough of her games, one minute treating him as if he were lower than a snake and the next going crazy in his arms. If it was deliberate, if it was real…

The Ice Princess had perfected teasing to an art. And he'd been performing like a trained seal.

A trite metaphor but there it was.

Okay. Enough was enough. He was tired of being played with. It was time to put an end to it and he knew exactly how he'd do it.

Take her to his bed. Nothing soft and gentle. He'd take her with brutal force, again and again, until she sobbed his name, until she clung to him, until whatever she'd really wanted was meaningless because by then, all she would want was him and everything he could do to her.

And when she finally lay spent beneath him, he'd get up, dress, toss a note for ten million euros on the dresser as if she were the world's most expensive whore because it was what she deserved for reducing him to this…

"Merda!"

Nick punched the mirror.

The glass shattered; drops of blood bloomed like tiny flowers on his knuckles. He cursed again, grabbed a towel, wrapped his hand in it.

And laughed.

Was this what it had come to? Was he so far gone he'd punch a mirror, indulge in a sexual fantasy that was not just bizarre but unreal, all because he'd somehow let a woman work her way under his skin?

He turned on the cold water, unwrapped his hand. The bleeding was minor. He could staunch it in the shower, which was exactly what he did.

"No more," he said grimly, raising his face to the spray.

He would meet Alessia this afternoon, but touring the vineyard wasn't on the agenda. Neither was the decorous dinner party she'd planned for tonight, no doubt to show her father's cronies what a tame *Siciliano* looked like.

To hell with being tame.

By evening, he'd have put an end to this thing. He'd be headed home. And the Ice Princess would have learned the consequences of taunting a man who carried the Orsini name.

He dressed casually. Black leather windbreaker, black T-shirt, faded jeans and sneakers.

At two minutes before one, he headed down the stairs. It

occurred to him that she might not be waiting for him, that maybe she'd figure she'd pushed the game too far.

Not that that would stop him.

He knew her rooms were in the same wing as his. It would only be a matter of slapping open doors until he found her.

But there she was, standing outside the villa, dressed as he was in a jacket, jeans, T-shirt and sneakers. Her hair was pulled back in the kind of ponytail it had been after her morning run. Had that been today? It seemed impossible.

He felt as if he had been here forever.

"Signore."

She looked up at him as he descended the last few marble steps. It was as if somebody had knocked the wind out of him. She was exquisite. How could he have ever thought her no more beautiful than other women who'd passed through his life? She didn't just have a lovely face, it was a face alive with intelligence. And the rest of her. The wide eyes a man could drown in. A long, lush body he had explored all too briefly...

Stop it, Nick told himself coldly. She couldn't go on with the game if he refused to participate, and it was time she got that message.

"Princess."

She looked him over from head to foot and gave a forced smile.

"I see you understand that touring the vineyard will not be, how do you say, a white-collar enterprise."

Nick's smile never reached his eyes. "Nothing about this afternoon will be white-collar, princess. I promise you that."

"I don't understand."

"What happened to calling me Nicolo?"

He saw her throat constrict. "I—I... Nothing happened. I just think, since this is all about business, we might wish to maintain a—"

"Never mind." He looked past her, toward the Jeep-like vehicle parked by the foot of the steps, and held out his hand. "The keys."

"*Scusi?*"

"I want your car keys."

"My car... Oh." Pink tinged her cheeks. "We shall be using a Massif, not the Mercedes, and I assure you, I will not have a driving problem on the vineyard's private ro—"

"The keys, Alessia."

She blinked. Then, slowly, she dropped the keys into his outstretched hand. Nick walked to the Massif, opened the door and motioned her inside. He didn't give a damn what they were using as long as she got the message.

He was in charge.

She gave him directions.

Take the dirt road behind the villa. Make a right at the top of the hill. A left at the crossroads. She babbled, too. Nervously, as if she sensed something was wrong, stuff about rootstock and slips and scions, about how, in ancient times, viniculturists didn't realize that cutting back a grapevine rather than letting it grow unrestrained would produce the best, the biggest crop of grapes.

Another time, he'd have found it fascinating. The only thing he knew about wine was either red or white and he liked drinking it with dinner; all these details, even now, piqued his curiosity.

But not enough to deter him from what would happen next, he told himself coldly. No way.

Eventually, Alessia fell silent.

He glanced at her. She sat rigid in her seat, hands tightly clasped in her lap.

"What's the matter?" he said brusquely. "Have you run

out of information you think even I might be capable of understanding?"

That made her jerk toward him.

"All right," she said, "all right, Mr. Orsini. Why not tell me the problem?"

Nick's mouth twisted. He pulled to a stop under a tree that stood at the end of a row of grapevines and shut off the engine.

"Why would there be a problem, *principessa?* You're the perfect tour guide."

Alessia looked at the man beside her. His tone was silky, his voice soft... And she was terrified. Something about him had changed. Where was the astute businessman of this morning's meeting? The acerbic guest who seemed no happier to be here than she was to be stuck with him?

Her throat constricted.

Where was the man who could not keep his hands off her, even though she didn't want him to touch her, to kiss her, to make her feel things she didn't understand?

Was this the man she had accused him of being, all along? The cold, heartless head of a crime syndicate, the kind of export her country had sent to America that made decent Italians cringe?

All at once, she didn't want to be alone with him in this isolated place.

She reached for the door handle. His hand closed hard on hers.

"Where are you going?"

"Outside. To—to see the vines. To make sure they've been properly prepared to endure over the winter."

Nick gave a harsh laugh. "Fascinating. The princess is also a farmer."

"I grew up here," she said stiffly. "When I was a child, I helped tend these vines. I helped pick the grapes. Besides, I thought you wanted to see things close-up. To walk among the vines and ask me about them."

"Is that what you thought, princess? That a man like me would bring you all the way out here to talk about grapes?"

She stared at him. "Yes. Yes, I did."

He started to tell her just how wrong she was. Then he took a long look at her. Her face was pale, her eyes deep and dark. Her lips trembled. Her hand, still locked under his on the door handle, was like ice.

Nick's jaw tightened.

She was frightened. Hell, that was what he'd wanted, wasn't it?

Wasn't it? he thought, and then he muttered an oath, lifted his hand from hers and flung his door open.

"What are you doing?"

"Exactly what you said I should be doing," he growled as he got out of the Massif. "I'm going to take a walk and ask you a lot of dumb questions."

"Questions are never dumb," she said in a small, girlish voice, and he knew then that whatever he'd intended to happen this afternoon was not going to happen.

She knew everything about grapes and wine.

She knew as much about them as he knew about investments and stocks.

What it came down to was that she knew a lot. And the more she talked, the more animated she grew. Her face took on color, her voice gained strength, even her eyes brightened.

Would another princess get down on her knees in the dirt with such enthusiasm, to brush away leaf litter and exclaim over the presence of a bud so small he had to get down on his knees with her to see it? Would another princess get a smear of dirt on her cheek and not give a damn? Would she talk with excitement and enthusiasm about cover crops, fall plantings of clover and peas, to minimize soil erosion during the winter?

Hell, Nick thought, watching her as she gently moved a bug aside, forget about princesses, would another woman do these things?

His sister, Izzy, maybe, because Iz was into plants and flowers and organic stuff, but a woman he dated?

No way.

He thought about the Sunday he'd taken the redhead he'd been seeing last summer to Central Park, after he'd grown weary of hearing her insist she wanted to watch him play football in the same kind of pick-up game he and his brothers had been part of for years.

What a disaster that had been.

Eeww, Nick, there are ants under this tree! Eeww, Nick, something just bit me! Eeww, Nick, there's a big thing with long legs crawling through the grass....

"She doesn't shut up, that big thing's gonna be me," Falco had growled.

The next Friday night, when they got together for beer and burgers at The Bar in Soho, Dante had exchanged glances with Rafe and Falco.

"So, how's the 'eeww' lady?" he'd said with a look of complete innocence.

"Eewt of the picture," Nick had replied, and Rafe had rewarded him with an ungentlemanly snort of beer.

Nobody would laugh, watching Alessia. She poked and prodded, sifted through decaying plant litter and when she was in the middle of earnestly explaining how, come spring, the cover crops would be plowed under and would help fertilize the earth, Nick told himself, *the hell with it,* and he reached for her, pulled her into his arms and kissed her.

She never so much as hesitated. Her arms went around his neck and she pulled him down to her.

She tasted of sun and soil, of the grapes and the seasons. She tasted of herself, warm and sweet, and of an impossible innocence.

Nick rolled her beneath him, cradled her face in his hands, kissed her again and again, each kiss deeper than the last. He could hear his blood roaring in his ears, could feel his heart pounding against hers.

"Nicolo," she whispered, all a woman could ever ask of a man in that one, softly spoken word, and he groaned and gathered her closer still, his hands in her hair, his body in the V of her legs, everything forgotten but this woman, this moment, this need.

His mouth was at her throat, his lips measuring the race of her pulse in its hollow, savoring the salty sweetness of her sun-warmed skin. Every muscle in his body had hardened; he could feel his erection swelling, swelling, swelling until it was almost painful.

His lips angled over hers. Tasting. Teasing. Her lips parted, letting him in. The taste of her made him groan. She was making little sounds, moans, whispers, and now she was arching against him, fingers digging into the hard muscles of his shoulders as her legs rose and closed around his hips. She rocked against him, her pelvis grinding against his swollen flesh, and he practically tore open her jacket, pushed up her T-shirt, found her braless, her breasts waiting for his lips, his teeth, and she gave a sharp cry, flung her head back, and his heart swelled with pleasure when he realized that she had come from that, just that, his mouth on her nipples.

"Nicolo." Her voice broke. She reached for him, cupped her hand over the denim that covered his straining flesh. Nick closed his eyes, let the feel of her touch send a shock wave through him and then, with his last bit of sanity, he took her hand from him, caught her other hand and held both between them, against his chest.

"No," she said in a fierce whisper, "no, don't stop! Nicolo, *per favore, io voglio—io voglio—*"

He kissed her. Swallowed her cries when what she wanted was what he had wanted all along, to bury himself deep, deep inside her.

But not here.

He wanted to be with her in a high-ceilinged room. To undress her as slowly as he could manage and still survive. To carry her to a bed covered in ivory linen, lay her down on it, see her golden hair loose against the pillow.

He wanted to watch her face as he touched her, explored her, all of her with his lips, his tongue, his hands.

He told her those things and watched her eyes blur.

"Tonight," she said brokenly, and he smiled.

"Yes, sweetheart. Tonight, we'll be lost in each other's arms."

"But not here. Not at the villa…"

"No." He kissed her again, softly, his mouth lingering against hers. "Not the villa, princess. I'll get us a place. The right place. I promise."

He rose to his feet, held out his hand. She took it and he drew her up beside him.

"We'll drive to Florence. Right now. And…" He looked at her. She was shaking her head. "What?"

"I forgot, Nicolo. The dinner."

"To hell with…" One glance at her face and he knew that was the wrong answer. "There's no way out of it, huh?"

"I planned it." She blushed. "It is what I do, you see? I represent people, bring them together, determine who will enjoy the company of whom. I know it is not an important occupation but—"

Nick silenced her with a kiss.

"If you do it, it's important." He brought her hand to his mouth and kissed her fingertips. "We can wait, sweetheart.

Didn't some wag once say that anticipation makes the heart grow fonder?"

Alessia wrinkled her brow. "Wag? You mean, as a dog moves its tail?"

He smiled. "That, too."

"I do not understand. Besides, it is absence that makes the heart grow fonder, not anticipation."

Nick drew her closer, cupped her bottom, heard her sweet gasp as she felt his hardness against her.

"Yeah," he said, his voice roughening, "but anticipation has its uses."

Alessia rose to him, her arms around his neck. She kissed him, touched the velvet tip of her tongue to his.

"*Sì,*" she whispered, and by the time they broke apart, it struck him as a minor miracle they hadn't turned into a column of flame.

CHAPTER EIGHT

ALESSIA had been to endless dinner parties, first as the daughter of a wealthy Florentine prince and in the last several years, as an up-and-coming associate at a publicity firm.

Some parties were dull. Some were interesting. The ones that involved her sometimes egotistically-challenged clients, a polite way of thinking of ones who were unsophisticated, were the most difficult.

She had to seem to be having fun even as she kept a sharp eye on everything.

Whatever kind of party it was, she'd long ago perfected the art of wearing a polite mask. She smiled, moved from group to group, carried on conversations about anything from art to Antarctica and did it all on autopilot.

And she was never nervous.

None of that applied tonight.

She was not just nervous, she was—there was no other word for it—a wreck.

Dressed and ready an hour early, staring at the clock in her bedroom, watching the minute hand drag around the dial didn't help and finally she gave up and headed downstairs.

Surely, there were things she could find in the drawing room, the dining room, to keep her busy.

But she couldn't.

Her father's household staff was well-trained, and she had arranged for her own coordinator to supervise things.

The drawing room was filled with light from half a dozen magnificent chandeliers; gold-rimmed champagne flutes and wine goblets that had been in the family for almost two centuries glittered on the enormous sideboard alongside an array of bottles that ranged from Cristal champagne to vintage Brunello di Montalcino, the incredibly expensive red wine for which the area was known.

The dining room table, set for twelve, was a masterwork of floral centerpieces, antique silver candelabra, her great-great-grandmother's china and sterling flatware that dated to the eighteenth century.

Alessia straightened a plate here, moved a fork there but the truth was, there was nothing for her to do....

Nothing except finally admit that her nerves had nothing to do with this dinner party and everything to do with Nicolo.

She had not seen him for hours.

They'd driven back to the villa from the hillside in silence. She hadn't known what to expect. Would he try to take her in his arms again? She was not ready for that. In fact, by the time they'd returned, she was stunned at what she'd said to him about wanting to be with him tonight and convinced she was not ready for anything to happen between them, now or ever.

The drive back had given her time to think.

What am I doing? she had thought.

Nothing sensible, that was certain.

Why would a logical woman even consider getting involved with a man she didn't know or want to know? Nicolo Orsini wore the right clothes and said the right things but that didn't change what he was.

Or what she became in his arms.

She had turned into someone else on that hillside, losing

her sense of self, of decorum, of—of morality. To have kissed him with wild abandon, to have begged him, *Dio,* begged him to take her…

All those thoughts had whirled through her head as they drove to the villa, but when they reached it, Nicolo had been the perfect gentleman. He'd helped her from the Massif, brought her hand to his mouth and lightly brushed a kiss over her knuckles.

Then he'd gone to his rooms and she had gone to hers. She had not seen him since, which was not what she'd anticipated. Despite their agreement that he would not make love to her in the Antoninni villa, she'd expected him to want to take her to his rooms, or to hers.

In fact, for the next couple of hours, each time she'd heard a footstep in the hall she'd felt her heart race, her mouth go dry because that footstep might be his, because she'd thought he might have been coming to her, coming *for* her to complete what they had started under that tree.

Just the thought had been enough to start her trembling.…

As she was trembling now.

Alessia went to the mahogany bar in the drawing room and poured herself a glass of wine.

The porcelain mantel clock softly ticked away the minutes. Soon, Nicolo would come through the doorway. She had learned enough about him to know that he was a man who understood the unwritten rules of business, and this was a business dinner. She had to remember that.

There was nothing of a social nature to it.

He would be on time. And she would tell him that what had almost happened today had been a mistake.

Her hand shook. Carefully, she set the glass on a small table. It would not do for the Princess Antoninni to greet her guests with wine stains on her gown.

Her gown.

Another mistake. Why had she let her friend, Gina, convince her to wear it? It was beautiful, yes, the most beautiful gown her friend, an up-and-coming young designer, had ever made.

But it was wrong for this occasion.

Last week, over a pick-up meal of cheese and salad in Gina's Roman *atelier,* she'd told her friend about the dinner party she had to preside over in honor of an American investor of her father's acquaintance.

"An American investor," Gina had said brightly. "Is he young and good-looking?"

"For all I know, he looks like an ape," Alessia had said glumly.

"But he's filthy rich?"

"Filthy, anyway."

Gina had laughed, hurried to a rack filled with clothes and yanked a gown from it.

"Ta-da," she'd said dramatically. "I have the perfect creation for you to wear. Take a look at this."

"This" was a stunning column of gold, embellished with tiny crystal paillettes.

"This man doesn't deserve anything so elegant," Alessia had said, but Gina had insisted she try it on.

"I told you," she'd said triumphantly, once Alessia had it on. "It is absolutely perfect."

Perfectly spectacular, Alessia had thought, looking at herself in the mirror. The cut of the halter-necked gown was deceptively simple—but the back of it dipped to the base of her spine and when she took a step, a slit in the skirt revealed a glimpse of leg from ankle to thigh.

Alessia had laughed.

"My job is to convince this man to give my father a lot of money, not seduce him."

"You'll dazzle him! He'll agree to anything. Between your title, that villa and this gown, you'll have him at your feet." Gina had wrinkled her nose. "Look, you don't like this guy and you haven't even met him. Think of what it'll be like to have him groveling."

It would be wonderful, Alessia had thought with sudden clarity.

She had taken the gown. And the stiletto-heeled gold sandals that went with it.

"The only thing you'll have to add is attitude," Gina had said with a wink, "but, hey, if you think like a princess, you won't have any trouble."

They'd both laughed, though Alessia could not imagine laughing now.

She picked up the glass again.

Very well.

She could, indeed, conjure up that regal attitude Gina had joked about. She would be polite but distant, pleasant but cool. And when the evening ended, she would tell this arrogant man that she had made a mistake on that hillside....

"Good evening, princess."

Alessia spun toward that slightly rough voice and her heart leaped into her throat.

"Nicolo," she said...and knew instantly that everything she'd just told herself was a lie.

She had not made a mistake this afternoon.

She wanted Nicolo Orsini to make love to her, and to hell with right and wrong.

She'd wanted him since he'd taken her in his arms as she wept so foolishly by the side of the road, she wanted him now, and nothing else mattered. He was everything she had ever let herself dream of in the darkest recesses of the night, and she was not going to walk away from what would surely never come into her life again.

"You are," he said softly, "incredibly beautiful."

She smiled. So was he. The leanly muscled body. The wide shoulders and long legs. The hard, angel-of-darkness face. The way he was looking at her.

"Thank you." She touched the tip of her tongue to her suddenly dry lips. "You look—you look very elegant in that tux."

It was an understatement of amazing proportions. He looked as if he'd just stepped out of a Ralph Lauren advertisement.

He smiled back at her. "I'm glad I packed it. A man could wear nothing else for an evening with a woman who looks the way you do tonight."

"It's the gown." Deliberately, as aware of him as if he were a lion and she were the female he was stalking, she turned in a little circle, just slowly enough to be sure he saw the low dip of the gown at her spine and the long, exposed length of her leg. "Do you like it?"

She watched his eyes narrow under his dark lashes, saw the tic of muscle in his jaw. Her entire body responded, pulse rocketing, skin flushing, bones threatening to turn to water. And when he started toward her, it was all she could do not to fly into his arms.

Kiss me, she thought, *kiss me now!*

Forget the carefully planned dinner, the guests, the cars even now pulling into the driveway, their headlights illuminating the drawing room.

But he didn't kiss her. He didn't touch her. He spoke to her, instead, and his words were more intimate than any caress.

"You're killing me," he said in a rough whisper.

Her heartbeat stuttered. "Am I?"

"You know damned well you are." He came even closer, so close she could feel the heat emanating from him, and ran a fingertip over her lips. "How am I going to keep my hands off you tonight?"

Alessia took a long breath.

"Don't keep them off me," she said, her voice trembling.

And then the butler entered the room and announced the arrival of the first guest.

The evening was never going to end.

Either that, or she was going to go up in flames before it did.

Her guests—her father's guests—were a polished, sophisticated group. Alessia knew he'd invited them to impress a potential investor. When he'd shown the guest list to her, she, who never gave a damn about impressing anyone, had coolly hoped for the same thing.

Better still, she'd hoped the American would be intimidated.

That was before she'd met Nicolo.

She knew now that no one and nothing would ever impress or intimidate him. Just as at the meeting earlier in the day, he was completely at ease, comfortable carrying on conversations about theater and travel and politics in English and in passable Italian.

Actually, it was he who directed conversations because, by the second course, her father's aristocratic and powerful cronies, and especially their ladies, were transfixed by the handsome, intelligent, interesting stranger seated to her right.

A good thing, too, because Alessia had virtually lost her ability to speak.

The reason?

Even as the guest of honor talked pleasantly with the others, even as he ate the elegant meal she had carefully organized, sipped the vintage Antoninni wines she had selected—

Even as he behaved with impeccable decorum—

Even then, he was touching her.

Nobody knew. Nobody saw. It was a hot, hidden secret shared only by the two of them—and it was the most exciting experience she could ever have imagined.

It had started back in the drawing room, after drinks were poured and hors d'oeuvres nibbled. A brush of his shoulder. A slide of his hand on her bare arm.

His hand placed on her back when dinner was announced.

It was a simple gesture, typical of most men escorting a woman to the table.

"Princess," Nicolo had said politely.

And spread his palm over her back.

Over her naked skin.

His warm, slightly calloused hand.

She'd caught her breath, looked up at him, saw his polite smile...saw the flame burning bright in his eyes.

In the dining room, he'd drawn her chair back from the table, his hand still on her. But as she took her seat, his fingers had dipped beneath the gold silk at the base of her spine in a swift, hot caress.

"Thank you," she'd said and he'd said, "You're very welcome, *principessa*," and she'd known, without question, that if he'd chosen that moment to lift her into his arms and carry her away, she'd have welcomed him doing it.

By now, he had touched her a dozen times.

His arm brushing hers when he turned his attention to another guest. His fingers, slipping against hers when she passed him the salt cellar.

But the game changed.

As the third course was served, she felt his hand on her leg.

A moan rose in her throat. She bit it back and did what she

could to smile brightly at the mayor, seated at the other end of the table, to pretend she knew what he was saying, but how could she? How could she when all she could think of was Nicolo's touch, his caress, the heat of his palm on her knee? Her thigh.

He was driving her wild.

And she loved it.

Dio, what was happening to her? She, the soul of propriety, the woman so steeped in the rules of etiquette that her employer always turned to her if questions arose.

She was hanging on to her sanity by a thread, and doing even that was becoming increasingly difficult. The room was spinning, and she knew it was not the wine. She had limited herself to the one glass before dinner and she had hardly touched the one that stood by her plate now.

Still, the room was spinning. She was breathing faster. She was hot, even though she knew the room itself was not.

Nicolo's hand moved. Caressed. His touch was... It was wicked magic. Rough. Silken. Warm.

She put her hand in her lap. Closed it over his. To stop him. Of course, to stop him... Or perhaps just so he would do this, yes, trace his thumb across her palm, fold his fingers through hers, move his hand and hers higher on her thigh...

"Is that not right, my dear?" a man two seats away said, smiling at her.

She stared at him. She could not put a name to the aristocratic face. He was—yes. He was an art dealer. She'd met him possibly a dozen times but his name had flown from her head. As for answering his question... How could she, when she had no idea what it meant?

I am, she thought with great clarity, *brain dead.*

The thought made her laugh. Apparently, it was the right thing to do because the others laughed, too.

"It's true, then," Nicolo said smoothly. "You really did bid on a Renoir at an auction at *Signore* Russo's gallery when you were seven years old?"

She flashed him a look filled with gratitude.

"Yes. I did. It was an accident, of course. I was there with my art tutor and I lifted my hand to scratch my nose."

More laughter. Nicolo leaned toward her. *"Brava, cara,"* he whispered, and she wanted to grab his head and kiss him.

The dessert course, at last.

Tiramisu. Tiny chestnut cakes. Antique gold-rimmed liqueur glasses of *strega* and *frangelico.* Espresso, in a coffee service as old as the villa. Laughter. Chatter.

And Nicolo, who had taken pity on her and had his hand on her thigh, but kept it still.

She could, at least, think.

What she thought about was him.

That she'd been prepared to despise him. That she'd been certain he would be rough and uncultured. That he would not be able to hold his own among truly civilized, worldly people.

Wrong. Wrong. Wrong.

He was wonderful. And sophisticated. And very much at ease in this sophisticated setting.

The women in the room couldn't take their eyes off him, and who could blame them? He was, without question, gorgeous. He'd have laughed at the word but it was accurate. The men hung on his every word. The mayor, the art dealer and another man, a wealthy eccentric, discreetly handed him their business cards.

He was charming to them all but she knew who really held his attention.

She did.

And when all these people finally left, when she and Nicolo would, at last, be alone...

The coffee cup shook in Alessia's hand. Carefully, she set it on the table.

She thought of what he had done all evening. How he had touched her. How his caresses had excited her.

She thought of how it would be, when everyone was gone and there was nothing to keep him from touching her more intimately, nothing to keep her from parting her legs, giving him deeper access to her body…

Dio.

Her pulse was thundering. She was wet and hot and she thought how readily she could give him that access now. She had only to place her hand under the table linen, place her fingers over his. Ease her thighs apart, guide his hand up and up and—

A little sound burst from her throat. Conversation stopped and she realized, to her horror, that every eye in the room was on her.

She told herself to say something. Anything. Her mind was blank. In desperation, she looked at Nicolo and saw that he knew what was happening to her.

Triumph blazed in his eyes.

Then, slowly, he moved his hand from her leg, made a fist of it and brought it to his mouth, smothering a polite but audible yawn. It was a good approximation of the sound she had made and everyone looked from her to him.

"I'm sorry," he said, with a charming smile. "*Mi dispiace.* I assure you, it isn't the company. This has been a wonderful evening. It's just that I've been on the go ever since early yesterday morning."

Everyone murmured their agreement. The guests tossed their napkins onto plates. Pushed back their chairs. Said *buona sera* and *arrivederci,* good-night and goodbye, and said it had been a delightful evening.

Nicolo politely helped her to her feet, held her elbow as they both accompanied everyone to the door. Car doors slammed. Headlights came on. A procession of elegant cars crawled down the long driveway.

And Alessia stood in the open front doorway, Nicolo beside her, smiling and waving as if she were simply a polite hostess seeing her guests off when, in truth, she was facing a moment of stark reality.

She and Nicolo were alone.

It was what she had longed for.

Now, it was what she feared.

The game they'd been playing had suddenly taken on a new dimension.

And it scared the hell out of her.

She didn't fear him. Never that. What she feared was herself. If he was not quite the man she'd thought, she was most certainly not the woman he thought, either.

Her behavior this afternoon, then this evening, surely would make him assume she was experienced in the ways of sex. Sophisticated. Worldly. A woman who was accustomed to pleasuring a man and being pleasured by him in return.

Nothing could have been further from the truth.

All of this was new to her. Everything she'd done, everything she'd initiated and responded to... She had never done anything even remotely like this before.

No, she wasn't a virgin. She was a modern woman. But what she knew about sex compared to what Nicolo must think she knew...

It was laughable.

She'd slept with a boy at school. He'd been as naive as she and, after a couple of weeks, they'd drifted back to being friends instead of lovers. Then, three years ago, there'd been an older man. A graphics artist. That had lasted all of a tepid month before he'd admitted he'd finally realized he preferred men.

Not much of a recommendation for a woman who'd spent

the last hours playing games with a man who, without question, had been with many, many women.

Beautiful women. Experienced women. He would expect things from her, with her, and she would surely disappoint him....

The taillights of the last departing vehicle vanished into the dark night. Nicolo's arms closed around her. He lowered his head to hers, pressed his lips to her ear.

"Princess," he said softly. "Whatever's going on in that lovely head?"

She could feel the heat of his body, the strength of it against her. She wanted to lean back into him. She wanted to turn and bring his mouth down to hers.

She wanted to run away before he discovered what a fraud she really was. Instead, she swallowed dryly. Forced a smile, even if he couldn't see it.

"Nothing," she said with false gaiety. "I'm just—you know, it's been a long day and—"

"Alessia." His hands cupped her shoulders and he turned her toward him. "I know something's wrong. What is it?"

She looked up at him, at that hard, handsome face, and then she dipped her head and lowered her lashes. "Nicolo. I think—I think we must talk."

He put his hand under her chin. Raised it until their eyes met.

"What I think," he said, his voice rough, "is that we've talked too much."

"We have not talked at all, Nicolo. We have—we have done other things—"

He framed her face. Lowered his mouth to hers. Kissed her tenderly, his lips moving on hers with growing hunger. He tasted of wine and coffee, of passion and of himself.

Alessia could feel her heart racing.

He tasted like every dream she'd ever had, every dream

she'd been afraid to dream. She held back, but only for a few seconds. Then she sighed and gave herself up to his kiss.

After a very long time, she put her hands against his chest.

"Nicolo," she whispered, and he lifted his head and looked down into her eyes.

"What is it, sweetheart?"

"I need to tell you… You must know…" She licked her lips. "What happened today was—it was—"

"It was the last thing either of us expected."

"Yes. That is true. My father… Your father…"

"They haven't got a thing to do with this."

"No. They do not. But—but you need to know… I must make something clear, Nicolo." *Dio,* she felt so foolish! Why was it so difficult to tell him that his expectations of her had little to do with reality? "What I'm trying to say is that you—you may have certain expectations of me—"

Nicolo swept his hands into her hair. She felt the pins that had secured it in a loose knot at the crown of her head come loose; golden strands cascaded over his fingers as he lifted her face to his and kissed her. Hard. Passionately. As if there had not been hours between those kisses under the tree on the hilltop and this one, as if they had never stopped tasting each other at all.

"The only expectation I have, princess, is that you'll let me make love to you until you tell me nothing else matters."

"Nothing does," she whispered. "Nothing could. I just—I do not want to disappoint you."

Disappoint him? What had happened tonight—Alessia's whisper just before they'd gone in to dinner, the way she'd looked at him throughout the meal, her increasing loss of control because of him, only him…

It had been more exciting than anything he'd ever experienced, and he was a man who had pretty much experienced everything.

"Truly, Nicolo, you must understand… I am not—I am not…" She drew a ragged breath. "When you touched me tonight, when you put your hand on me…" Her voice broke. "I almost—I almost—"

Jesus, she was going to kill him! Nick leaned his forehead against hers and gave a soft, ragged laugh.

"I know, sweetheart. Me, too."

She looked up at him, her cheeks flaming. "Truly?"

"Yeah." Another ragged laugh. "And wouldn't your old man's fancy friends have loved that?"

"Because—because all I could think of was what would happen if—if you touched me more. If you moved your hand, only a little—"

"Enough," Nick growled, and drew her hard against his side, silencing her with a kiss as he hurried her down the wide marble steps to a gleaming red Ferrari.

"Mine," he said, in answer to her unspoken question. "Delivered here an hour ago." He opened the passenger door, one arm curved around her as he did, with such blatant masculine possessiveness that she felt her knees go weak.

"Your seat belt," he said, once he was behind the wheel, the words an imperious command.

Alessia complied, though her hands trembled. The car gave a throaty roar as he turned the key.

"Where are we going?"

"To a place where we can be alone without the ghosts of your father or mine looking on."

Then he leaned toward her, gave her one last, deep kiss before he stepped hard on the gas and the Ferrari leaped into the night.

CHAPTER NINE

NICK drove fast, his hands light and sure on the steering wheel.

He let the Ferrari take the winding roads into the dark hills like the thoroughbred it was.

They weren't going very far. Twenty miles. Fifteen minutes, the Realtor had said, twenty at the most.

The road ahead climbed higher. Nick downshifted and thought fifteen minutes would be about all he could manage.

He'd wanted women before. Why not? He was a man in the prime of life. But he'd never wanted a woman like this, with a need so strong, so powerful, that having her was all he could think about.

It had taken him most of the afternoon, making calls on his cell phone to make arrangements for tonight. He rarely thought about the fact that he had, to put it bluntly, an almost unfathomable amount of money and the connections that went with it, but there were times having money and those connections could change everything.

First, he'd phoned a Ferrari dealer in New York, who had phoned a Ferrari dealer in Florence. Then he'd called a banker pal in London who'd called a Realtor in Siena who'd called a Realtor in Florence...

It had all been time-consuming, but he'd finished with an

hour to kill before a dinner party he wanted to attend about as much as a vampire would want to have a vegetarian lunch.

Taillights winked just ahead. Nick checked his mirror, swung out and passed the vehicle as the speedometer neared ninety.

That final hour had been an eternity.

A voice inside had kept saying, *What are you waiting for? Find her. Push her against the wall. Ruck up her skirt, unzip your fly, hold her wrists high over her head and drive into her while she sobs your name and comes and comes and comes....*

Crazy, he'd told himself, even to have thought that way.

Life was all about self-control.

He'd learned that growing up, when being a son of Cesare Orsini had made him fair game for every TV newshound in New York. He'd perfected it in combat, especially in clandestine ops where self-discipline could be the difference between life and death. It was the single most important factor that had made him the kind of gambler who won far more often than he lost, at cards and then as a financial decision-maker at Orsini Investments.

And, of course, relationships with women, in bed and out, were all about a man exercising self-control.

And why he'd been thinking about relationships when a minute earlier he'd been thinking about Sex, Sex with a capital *S,* had been beyond him to comprehend.

So he'd taken an endless shower, let the cold water beat down until he could think straight. Then he'd dressed in the tux he'd thought to bring with him, looked in the mirror at the image of a civilized man about to deal with a woman in a civilized way...

Until he got downstairs and saw Alessia.

The beautiful face. The gorgeous body. The gown that was an invitation to sin, the take-me stiletto heels.

How am I going to keep my hands off you? he'd said.

Her sexy-as-hell response had sent the civilized man inside him packing.

Somehow, they'd made it through dinner, playing a game so hot he was amazed they hadn't set the place on fire. That he'd been forced to carry on intelligent conversation while he touched her had added to it.

And then that last moment, when he'd brought her to the brink...

A muscle knotted in his jaw.

He glanced at Alessia. She hadn't spoken since she'd asked him where he was taking her. She sat very straight, hands folded in her lap, gaze straight ahead. Was she imagining what would happen next? Was her body softening as she pictured him touching her?

Or was she worried that she wouldn't—how had she put it? That she wouldn't live up to his expectations?

Was she really that naive? Or simply clever?

He told himself it didn't matter.

Hell. Why lie to himself? It mattered. A lot. When they were finally alone, what if what he did to her, did with her, was new to her? What if he was the first man to teach her things that would make her moan and beg him to end the exquisite torment, as she had today on the hilltop?

Dammit!

Nick shifted his weight in the seat. If he kept this up, they might never make it to the villa he'd rented.... And, thank God, there it was, just ahead and exactly as the Realtor had described. A narrow gravel road, leading through an open iron gate. A stand of gnarled olive trees. And in the distance, the lights of a stone house.

Villa Riposante.

And not a minute too soon.

* * *

Alessia trembled as she stepped from the car.

"Here," Nicolo said, shrugging off his jacket and wrapping it around her shoulders. "This should keep you warm until we're inside."

She nodded, though he was wrong.

She was not cold, she was terrified. Not of him. That fear was long since gone. She was terrified of herself, of the awful knowledge that no matter what he'd said, she knew she was going to disappoint him.

She had no idea where they were, only that they were in the hills high above Villa Antoninni and that this place, this beautiful stone villa, could only have been found on such short notice by a man who could ask whatever he wished of the world and get it.

He put his arm around her, led her up the stone steps to the door. The key—big, brass, old—was under a thick rush doormat. Nicolo inserted it in the lock, turned it, the heavy wood and brass door swung open...

"Nicolo." She sounded breathless and she was. This was a mistake. A mistake. To have led him on, to have let him think... "Nicolo," she said again, this time with urgency. "Listen to me—"

All at once, she was being swept up in his arms.

"Stop thinking," he said in a rough voice. "Stop worrying. Just let the night happen."

He elbowed the door shut behind him as he carried her into the villa. Alessia wound her arms around his neck and buried her face against his throat. She could feel his heart thudding against hers.

The villa was softly lit. And beautiful, what she saw of it over his shoulder. A frescoed ceiling. A floor of pale gray stone. A steep wooden staircase and at the top, a stream of ivory moonlight that led into a room lit by tapers in tall silver candlesticks. A fire glowed on a slate hearth; orchids rose like graceful ballerinas from crystal vases on the dresser and the night tables....

The night tables that framed the bed.

The bed.

A canopied bed, draped in endless, drifting layers of pale pink silk.

Nicolo let her slide down the length of his body to stand on her feet. She caught her breath at the feel of his erection. He took her hand; she thought he was going to put it against his fly. Instead, he brought her fingers to his lips and kissed them.

There was something so sweet, so touching, in the simple gesture that it made her throat constrict.

He turned away. Closed the door. When he looked at her again, his expression was unreadable. She waited for him to reach for her, to touch her, but he did nothing, he only stood still, watching her through narrowed eyes.

She understood.

He had done his part.

The car. The villa. The flowers. The fire on the hearth. It was all very romantic, but now it was her turn. She wasn't ready but that wasn't his problem, she thought, and she took a deep breath, raised her arms, reached for the tiny loops and hooks that were at the back of her gown's halter neck.

"No."

Her eyes flew to his. He moved toward her, caught her wrists, brought her hands to her sides.

"I want to undress you," he said in a husky whisper.

Could a man say anything more wonderful to his lover? Alessia's heart lifted. Her lips curved in a smile.

"It is what I want, too," she said softly, and Nick drew her to him and kissed her, his mouth moving slowly against hers, very slowly. Going slowly was what he wanted for her. Still, he might be pushing too hard, too fast… And then she groaned, rose to him, opened her mouth to his…

And he stopped thinking.

How could a man think when a woman's taste was so sweet? When she felt so soft, so right? The press of her breasts against his chest. The warmth of her arms around his neck. And those sexy high heels meant that her hips were against his.

He slid one hand down her back. Felt the silken texture of her skin. Cupped her bottom, lifted her into him, and she sighed his name against his lips.

"Nicolo."

Just that, nothing more, and yet he felt as if his heart might leap from his chest.

"Yes, sweetheart," he murmured, and he turned her in his arms, swept her long fall of golden hair aside and fumbled for the loops and buttons at the gown's halter neck, knowing those tiny bits of gold and cotton were all that kept her from him.

His fingers felt big. Clumsy. Undoing the buttons seemed to take forever.…

And then, at last, they were undone.

The bodice of the gown slipped down.

She caught it and held it against her. Nick didn't try to stop her. Instead, he bent his head and put his lips to the tender skin he had uncovered just at the nape of her neck. A soft kiss. Another. The faint nip of his teeth and she moaned. Her head fell forward; her hair tumbled over her shoulders. Nick trailed the tip of his tongue along her sweet, heated flesh, then kissed his way down her spine.

Alessia's moans became soft whimpers of pleasure and when he could take no more, he cupped her shoulders and turned her toward him.

Her head lifted. Her eyes met his and he felt his heart turn over. Everything a man could possibly dream was in her eyes, desire and need and something more, something that made him murmur her name, lift her to him and take her mouth with growing hunger.

She kissed him back, her teeth closing lightly on his bottom lip.

Adrenaline flooded his blood.

He took control of the kiss. Deepened it, until she was clinging to him. His lips moved to her jaw, her throat, her shoulder. She gasped, shuddered, her hands drove into his hair and the bodice of the gown, now forgotten, fell away.

"Alessia." His voice was hoarse. "*Mia bella* Alessia..."

His hands shook as he hooked his thumbs into the gown's deep V at the base of her spine and slowly eased it down. The silk whispered over her hips. Her buttocks. Her thighs. Nick groaned and let it slip from his hands to become a soft circlet of gold around those sexy stilettos.

"Nicolo," she whispered.

"Yes, baby."

"Nicolo. Please."

The word was a sob. A plea. Nick felt his heart thud. He knew what she was asking, knew, too, that he was as close to finishing this before it really began as he had ever been in his life. He could feel everything within him tightening, coalescing, centering low in his belly as he looked at her glittering eyes, her kiss-stung lips, the black lace thong between her thighs.

A shudder went through his big body.

He wanted to tear the thong from her, bare her to his hands, his eyes, take her again and again and again....

Instead, he took a harsh breath, wove his fingers through hers. Helped her step free of the gown. Let go of her hands, reached for the thin silk band of the lace thong, drew it down and down and down...

And looked at her. Just looked at her.

The sight almost stopped his heart.

His princess had the face of a Botticelli angel. The body of a Venus. Small, rounded, up-tilted breasts crowned with nipples the color of the palest of pink roses. A narrow waist rising from curved hips. Endless legs, topped by a cluster of honey-colored curls. She was exquisite, a man's most perfect dream....

A man's most perfect desire.

Her breathing was quick and shallow. Her eyes were feverish, the pupils deep and dark. She started to raise her arms to cover herself, but Nick caught her wrists and brought her hands gently to her sides.

"You are beautiful," he said. "More beautiful than I could ever have imagined."

Her lips curved and he leaned toward her, brought his mouth to hers, kissed her and kissed her until she murmured his name, again and again.

"Yes," he whispered, "yes, sweetheart, yes..."

Nick watched her face as he raised his hands and cupped her breasts. Her breath hissed at his touch. God, oh, God, the softness of her breasts against his palms. The delicate weight. His thumbs rolled over her nipples.

She cried out; she trembled, her hands dug into his shoulders.

"Do you like that?" he said hoarsely, his eyes locked on her face. "Tell me what you like, sweetheart," he whispered, and he dipped his head, licked one lovely furled tip, then sucked it into his mouth.

Alessia's knees buckled and Nick swept her into his arms and took her to the bed. A bed that might have been designed with his princess in mind.

The silky coverings were as soft as her skin, the blues

as vivid as her eyes. She lay back and her hair fell over the pillows like spun gold.

His heartbeat skittered.

She was more than beautiful. She was exquisite.

Her arms rose, reached for him. He obliged, came down on the bed beside her, kissed her, then ran his hand lightly over her from throat to breast to belly. She caught his hand. Lifted it to her lips and kissed his fingers. Touched the tip of her pink tongue to his palm.

A groan tore from his throat.

He wanted to look at her forever. He wanted to caress her, to spend an eternity exploring her...

He wanted to tear off his clothes and bury himself inside her.

"Please, Nicolo," she said brokenly. *"Per favore, Nicolo mio..."*

Ah, dear God, he was going to explode.

He could feel it happening. The heat, gathering low in his belly. His scrotum tightening, his aroused sex now so hard, so swollen it was almost painful.

He wanted to end her torment and his but somehow he held back. He had to make this last. Last forever. Even now, his brain barely functioning, he understood that such a thing was impossible and yet, he wanted to find a way to make it be true....

And, suddenly, his mind achieved a terrible clarity. For all his careful planning, he had forgotten one thing.

Condoms.

He had no condoms! How could he been so stupid? The thought of stopping now...

"Nicolo?"

"Yes." Nick framed her face in his hands. "Sweetheart. Alessia. I forgot..." Silently, he cursed himself for being such a fool. This wouldn't be the most romantic of questions but it had to be asked. He could only pray she had the right answer. "Are you on—"

"The pill." She blushed. That she could blush as she lay naked in his arms only heightened his arousal. "*Sì*. There is no need to worry. I am—"

His kiss was deep and drugging. Her response was wild and he gave up any final attempt at rational thought, came down to her and gathered her in his arms. She clasped the back of his head, dragged his mouth to hers and kissed him, drew the tip of his tongue into her mouth. He rolled her beneath him, brought his lips to her breast, drew a budded nipple between his teeth, and her cry shattered the night.

She said something in Italian. The words were soft and hot and desperate. They needed no translation.

Nick reared back. Tore off his clothes and Alessia reached for him, wrapped her arms around his neck and pressed her body to his.

He shuddered.

There was so much he wanted to show her. To teach her. But she was sobbing his name, arching like a bow against him and he tried, God, he tried, entering her slowly, as slowly as he could, and when she screamed in ecstasy, he was lost.

He drew back, then drove deep again and again and again until she was wild beneath him, until he could feel the contractions of her womb....

Nick threw back his head and followed his princess into the starry night.

He slept.

She did, too, curled in his arms, her head on his shoulder, her hair silky against his lips.

The night grew chilly. He awoke just long enough to pull the duvet over them both.

"Mmm," she sighed, and he gathered her closer, told

himself he wouldn't wake her, that he would only hold her, like this. Stroke his hand down the length of her spine, like this. Repeat the caress until she made that soft little sound again and now he would rise over her, just a little, bring his mouth to hers, kiss her softly, lightly, gently…

She sighed again, and he rolled her gently on her back. Absolutely, he would let her sleep. She had to be exhausted after the last couple of days. All he would do was kiss her a little more.

Her closed eyes. Her temples.

Her mouth. Her delectable mouth.

"Nicolo?"

Her lashes fluttered. Her eyes opened. "Nicolo," she whispered. Her arms went around him. "Nicolo," she sighed, her mouth warm and sweet against his, clinging to his, and then, somehow, his lips were on her throat. Her shoulder.

Her breasts.

Her nipples, delicately beaded, their taste like honey against his tongue.

His kisses drifted lower. And lower. He heard her breath catch.

"Nicolo? What are you…?"

"Nothing," he said, his lips at her navel. "Nothing at all."

"Oh. Oh, Nicolo! You can't—you shouldn't…" She gave a soft cry as he parted the delicate petals of her labia. Inhaled her essence. Sought out the delicate bud that awaited him.

Her cry rose into the night.

He kissed her there again. And again. Stroked her. Caressed her. And when finally he entered her, this time he did as he had hoped to do the first time, entered her slowly, slowly enough to bring them both to the edge of eternity, to that moment that is part death, part paradise.

And when it was over, Nicolo gathered his princess in his arms, against his heart, and knew that whatever it was he had found in the last forty-eight hours was more than he had ever anticipated....

And more than some men found in a lifetime.

CHAPTER TEN

ALESSIA woke to sunlight, the smell of coffee...

And a heart-stopping view of her lover.

Nicolo had just walked out of the en suite bathroom, drops of water crystallizing on his tanned skin. He was toweling his hair. Which left the rest of him naked. Gloriously, unashamedly naked.

Heat swept through her veins. Such a magnificent sight!

Her lover was beautiful. So beautiful. Until now, she had not had the chance to look at him, really look at him, and appreciate the sight. He'd made love to her again and again through the long, wondrous night. The stroke of his hand on her, of his mouth, the feel of him against her...and under her, she remembered with a soft catch of her breath—all of those incredible things were now hers, forever, imprinted in her mind and on her flesh.

But she had not had the chance to see how perfect he was.

Now, she could look her fill. Without embarrassment, because he had no idea she was awake. And, oh, he was a sight to behold. The muscled shoulders and arms. The dark whorl of hair on his chest. The way it arrowed down his flat, hard belly, tapered to his navel, then flared out again as it surrounded that part of him that was flagrantly, unashamedly male.

Alessia was a child of the city of Florence. She had grown

up virtually surrounded by magnificent works of art, including Michelangelo's *David*. She'd been stunned by the artistry of the great marble sculpture…and, the same as generations of other adolescent girls, amazed by the depiction of all that intimate masculine beauty. Of course, she had stared. What teenager wouldn't?

Now, for the first time in years, she thought of the statue again.

David had nothing on her Nicolo.

Nothing at all.

The thought was totally unlike her. It made her giggle.…

A mistake.

Nicolo took the towel from his head and looked at her. "Just what every man wants," he said. "Laughter from his woman, first thing in the morning."

His woman. The words filled her with joy but the expression on his face filled her with laughter and she couldn't help it, she snorted back another giggle.

He raised his eyebrows, draped the towel around his neck—his neck, she noticed, not his hips—and came slowly toward her. "The sight of me without a stitch on is amusing?"

He looked deadly serious. Had she actually offended him?

"No, of course not. It is only that—that I was imagining the statue."

"What statue?"

"*David*. You know the one. And I was thinking that you—that you and *David*—"

"Go on."

She couldn't. Oh, she couldn't. This was embarrassing. It was humiliating. It was—

She gasped as Nicolo flung himself down beside her, grabbed her wrists, hauled them high over her head…and kissed her. She could feel his lips curving against hers.

"Ah-ha," he said in a mock-growl, "the lady is a student of art."

"You are laughing at me," she said, trying to sound stern.

"Not if you tell me who won."

Dio, now she knew she was blushing! "Who won what?" she said, trying for innocent indignation and knowing she wasn't succeeding.

"You know exactly what. *David* and me. Hey, you're talking to a guy who has two sisters. Anna and Izzy spent a summer touring Europe when they were, I don't know, maybe fourteen and fifteen. The trip was supposedly all about art."

"Art is an important part of a young woman's education," Alessia said primly.

"Uh-huh." Nick grinned at the look on his princess's face. She was doing her best to sound proper. Not an easy thing when laughter glinted in her eyes. "From what they said, or maybe from the way they said it, it took my brothers and me ten seconds to figure out that the highlight of their visit to Florence was that statue."

"*David* is a revered work of art," Alessia said, trying not to laugh.

"At least tell me Dave and I came out even. Hey, you've got to keep in mind, Dave is, what, twenty feet tall?"

"Seventeen," she said, and another giggle burst from her lips.

"Yeah, well, I've seen some pretty interesting sculptures, too." He nuzzled her throat, loving the delicious mingled scents of woman and sleep and sex. It had taken all his determination not to wake her with kisses this morning but he'd made love to her so many times during the night that he'd felt a twinge of guilt at the thought of depriving her of a little more sleep. "The *Venus de Milo.* The *Winged Victory.*"

Alessia pulled one hand free and swatted his shoulder. "The *Winged Victory* has no arms and no head."

"Trust a woman to notice something like that." Nick nipped lightly at her shoulder, heard her soft intake of breath as he shifted against her. "The point is, you win, hands down."

"What is this hands-down thing?"

He pulled back. Not far, just enough so he could see all of her face.

"It means," he said, "that you're a hundred times more beautiful."

She smiled. Stroked a dark strand of hair back from his forehead.

"Liar," she whispered.

"A million times more beautiful," he said softly.

He kissed her. Moved over her. Kissed her again and again, until laughter had been replaced by passion.

"Nicolo," Alessia whispered, "Nicolo, *mio amante*."

She had called him her lover. And that was what he was, he thought fiercely, what he wanted to be, what he would be....

And then he stopped thinking and let the world slip away.

The day was overcast.

It didn't matter.

They ran a mile together, returned, showered and made love. Then they ate a huge meal—the villa came complete with staff—and talked and laughed and talked some more.

Hands linked, they strolled the grounds. The place was all Nick had hoped for. Quiet. Isolated. Nothing but a soft breeze that swept through the ancient olive trees, a small vineyard and, over a rise, a stable and half a dozen horses grazing in a paddock.

He watched Alessia as she petted the animals, watched their reactions to her touch. One big stallion snorted, tossed his head, then leaned into her hand.

I know how you feel, pal, he thought, and when his princess turned and smiled up at him, he cupped her face and kissed her.

"Happy?" he asked, after they'd climbed a hill, reached the top and found a view that stretched for miles.

"Very happy. To be here, in such a beautiful place with you… How did you find it?"

"Pay the price and maybe I'll tell you."

"It all depends on the price."

"A kiss," he said, swinging her toward him.

Alessia fluttered her lashes. "You drive a hard bargain, *signore.*" She stood on her toes and planted a quick kiss on his cheek.

"You call that a kiss?" Nick grabbed her, dipped her back over his arm and she offered an appropriate shriek. "This," he said, "is a kiss!"

She laughed. So did he. But the kiss went from melodramatic to passionate to sweetly, achingly tender, and Nick sank down on the grass and drew her down beside him.

She sighed and laid her head against his shoulder, and he tried to figure out how he could ever have thought her cold and imperious.

The truth was that she was warm and giving.

She was amazing.

He had never enjoyed being with a woman as much as he enjoyed being with his princess. "Enjoy" was the wrong way to describe it. A man could enjoy a fast car. A deal he'd successfully concluded. But what he felt about Alessia was more intense. More vital. What he felt was more like—more like—

Nick blinked.

Easy, he told himself. Just slow down. Relax.

Alessia was bright. She was funny. She was beautiful. He liked talking with her, sparring with her, having sex with her, but sex was what it was. Incredible sex, especially considering that she'd had been concerned about meeting his expectations. She'd made it sound as if she was inexperienced.

Maybe. But she was the most responsive lover imaginable.

And she was on the pill. A good thing, considering that he'd managed to think of everything but protection.

But...

But, why was she on birth control? Better still, why did it bother him? Because it did. That she was using something was, as he'd just told himself, a damned good thing. Otherwise, what would they have done last night besides drive each other half-crazy?

Besides, he wasn't a male chauvinist. He was all in favor of women having the same rights as men, in sex and in everything else.

Except, suppose she was on the pill because she already had a lover. Then what? Was he sharing her with a man who had the right to touch her as intimately as he had, to explore her body's dark, sweet secrets?

Last night, she'd cried out his name.

Was there some other name she had cried out last week—and would cry out again, once he was gone?

He couldn't imagine that. She was not a woman who would go from one man to another. And despite her responsiveness, despite her being sophisticated enough to keep herself protected against an unplanned pregnancy, her reactions to what happened between them in bed were, for lack of a better word, innocent.

Her sighs. Her moans. They spoke not of knowledge but of wonder.

The first time he'd put his mouth between her thighs, she'd been shocked. *No,* she'd said, *no!* Not in fear. In stunned amazement that he would do such a thing. But he'd gone on kissing her, tasting her, and her shock had given way to ecstasy and she'd sobbed his name, come apart as he licked her....

Hell.

If he kept this up, he was going to turn her toward him, strip off her clothes, make love to her right here, on this hilltop....

"Nicolo?"

Nick cleared his throat. "Yes, sweetheart?"

"Would it be terrible of me to ask you...to ask you to take me back to the villa?"

His heart leaped. "If that's what you want—"

"What I want," she said in a low voice, "what I want, Nicolo, is you."

Her honesty made her blush. That, coupled with what he saw in her eyes, was almost his undoing. He rose, brought her up beside him, took her in his arms and kissed her. Then he took her back to the villa, to the bed, *their* bed, and as she sighed his name and welcomed him into her warmth, all his doubts vanished.

She belonged to him.

Only to him.

She fell asleep in his arms.

Nick lay holding her, his eyes fixed on the ceiling. The sun was sinking behind the hills, casting long shadows over the room. The day was ending and, damn, he hated to see it happen. Soon, it would be time to leave here and return to the Antoninni villa.

To reality.

Alessia stirred, sighed in her sleep and cuddled closer. His arms tightened around her. When she awoke, he'd tell her he'd made some decisions.

He would lend her father the money to restore the winery and the vineyard to their glory days, free of restrictions. He would not demand control of it. He'd said that in anger that was long gone.

And he wouldn't remain here for two weeks. It was an impossibility. He'd really known it when he'd said it but, again, anger had overrun common sense. He had commitments in New York. Meetings. Clients. There was no way to ignore any of it.

So, no, he wouldn't stay....

But he'd come back.

He'd make that very clear to her. Not next weekend—now that he thought about it, he had a trip to Chicago scheduled. And not the weekend after. There was something in his calendar about an appointment in Beijing. But he'd come back....

The muscle in his jaw knotted.

Planning ahead put a different spin on things. It made things complicated. Made them more serious.

And as much as he—as he liked Alessia, this wasn't serious. Intense, sure. But serious...?

Nick frowned. Why think about that now? He was here and so was she, lying warm and soft against him. Her hair smelled of sunshine, her skin of a perfume all her own.

His body hardened.

He wanted her again.

He drew her nearer, brushed his mouth lightly over hers, and she stirred.

"Mmm," she sighed.

"Mmm, indeed," he whispered and when she opened her eyes and smiled, he gave up thinking altogether and lost himself in her arms again.

Hours went by.

They slept. Showered. Had espresso on a broad terrace overlooking the olive groves and by then, it was too late to go back to the Antoninni winery.

And, really, what was the rush?

Nick had figured on flying back to New York tomorrow morning, but he could just as easily leave in the afternoon. No way was he going to risk spending hours stuck at an airport this time and since the Orsini plane was in use by one of his brothers—he'd phoned and checked—he'd be using a chartered flight. One of the advantages of renting a private plane was that it flew at your convenience, not that of others.

He made a quick call to the Realtor and arranged to keep the villa for another night.

The cook produced a meal as good as any in a five-star restaurant. Soup. Salad. Pasta. Fish. A chocolate gelato that made Alessia lick her lips in a way that meant Nick just had to taste the rich ice cream, but on her tongue, not his. The butler produced a bottle of red wine; apparently, the guy recognized *la principessa* as a representative of the famous Antoninni Vineyards and solemnly handed her the cork. Equally solemnly, she sniffed it, then sniffed the scant inch of wine he poured, tasted it, savored it, thought about it…

And burst out laughing at the look on Nick's face, which changed her from wine snob into gorgeous woman in a heartbeat, and made him lean across the candlelit table to steal a wine-flavored kiss and to hell with the butler watching.

"Tell me about New York," she said, over espresso.

"Haven't you ever been there?"

"Oh, yes. Many times." She looked at him and smiled. "I want you to tell me about *your* New York. The places that are special to you."

Nick obliged.

He told her about a museum called the Cloisters, in upper Manhattan. The narrow streets of Soho, at the other end of the island. The saloon he and his brothers had bought there, years back, to keep it from being turned into a cocktail lounge.

That had made her laugh. "You said 'cocktail lounge' as if it were a curse."

"Turning an honest-to-God bar into a place where people order drinks you have to make with a blender *is* a curse," he said, and this time it was Alessia who leaned across the table and stole a kiss.

"I would love to see the New York you have described."

Nick didn't have to think about it. He reached for her hand, ran his thumb lightly over her fingers. "I want you to see it."

She smiled. "I would like that, Nicolo."

He would like it, too—and here they were, back at the same logistics problem he'd been thinking about a couple of hours ago. Okay. He'd have to work something out. Make plans, fairly long-range plans, to keep the relationship going...

Hell. Was that what it was? A relationship?

Well, no.

It was an affair. And yeah, there was a difference...

"...a big family."

He blinked. "What?"

"This morning, you said two sisters. And now you talk of your brothers. A big family. That is nice."

Amazing. He'd told her more personal stuff in a handful of hours than he'd ever told another woman no matter how long they'd been involved.

Nick swallowed hard. *Involved?*

"How many brothers do you have?"

"Three." Her look of astonishment lightened the mood. He laughed, touched his index finger to the tip of her nose. "Hey, we're *Siciliano*. What can I say?"

Her smile wavered. "Of course."

Nick cocked his head. "Meaning?"

"Nothing." She looked down at her glass, as if her interest

had suddenly been captured by the wine. "It is only that—that I had almost forgotten who—who—"

"Who I am," he said with cool belligerence. So much for personal stuff. "Right. Not just a Sicilian. A Sicilian named Orsini."

Alessia shook her head. She raised her eyes to his and he saw that she was blinking back tears. So, what? All that had happened between them meant nothing when you got down to basics. It was the princess and the peasant again, right where they'd started.

"No," she said in an unsteady whisper. "Nicolo, you cannot be—you cannot possibly be—"

A crook. A thug. A member of *la famiglia*. Right. He was none of those things. Now was the time to tell her what a less pigheaded man would have told her from the beginning. That he was an investor. A financial analyst. That he was as legitimate as Mother Teresa—okay, maybe not quite as legitimate as that, but he could surely tell her he was an honest guy who'd worked hard for what he had, that he'd turned his back on his father and everything he represented before he'd been old enough to vote...

Instead, some terrible streak of Sicilian perversity drove him on.

"What if I can be?" he said tonelessly. "What if told you that I am exactly the man you think I am? What would you do then?"

Alessia stared at him for an endless moment. He waited and wondered why he should be waiting, and then the tears she'd tried to stem spilled down her cheeks.

"I would say, it does not matter," she said brokenly. "I might go straight to hell for it, Nicolo, but I would say, 'It does not matter what you are.' You are *mio amante,* you are my lover, and I want you, I want you, I want—"

A heartbeat later, she was in Nick's arms. And as he kissed her, he realized there was no way in the world he would fly back to New York tomorrow.

CHAPTER ELEVEN

WHEN she was a little girl, Alessia had been taught by a seemingly endless procession of tutors and nannies.

At first, with a small child's belief in the infallibility of adults, she'd believed that each of them knew everything there was to know about the world.

A stern-faced woman named *Signorina* Felini taught her otherwise.

Signorina Felini had been hired specifically for her supposed expertise in science. Almost from the start, things went badly.

When she could not explain why the moon was sometimes full and sometimes barely a sliver, Alessia went to the villa's huge library, found a book on astronomy and, with a little diligent research, found the answer. The *signorina* was not pleased, nor was she pleased when Alessia corrected her version of why there were different seasons in the year.

The end came when Alessia asked what would it would be like if an astronaut fell into the sun.

"Such a thing is impossible," said *Signorina* Felini brusquely.

"You mean, he'd burn up before he reached it?" Alessia asked.

Her teacher frowned. "The sun is up there. All else is down here. That is why no one could possibly fall into it."

Alessia's mother happened to overhear the conversation. Nella Antoninni knew little about the sun and the sky but she knew enough to put an end to the *signorina's* employment. A new tutor with a provable degree in earth sciences took her place.

One night, after Alessia and Nicolo had been together for almost two weeks, she awoke to his kisses on the nape of her neck, the sexy stroke of his fingers on her nipples. And just before she lost herself in passion she suddenly thought, *This is how it would be to fall into the sun.*

Flame. Heat. Knowing that you were burning up and not caring, never caring because soon you would be reborn...

Except, she thought the next day, as she put her foot into the palm of her lover's hand and let him help her into the saddle of the mare she'd taken to riding, except she had already been reborn.

She was Nicolo's lover. And he was hers.

Her lover. And—and her love.

The realization swept through her, left her breathless. She clung to the mare's reins, watching as Nicolo swung onto the back of a black stallion, her eyes, her very soul, taking in his beauty, his grace, his power, his air of command. He was sexy and gorgeous, a man any woman would want....

But love wasn't possible. That couldn't be what she felt. Love didn't come this quickly, not unless it happened in fairy tales and this was the real world, not a fairy tale. She couldn't love him. She was confusing love with passion. With desire. And yes, she desired him all the time. His arms around her. His mouth on her. His hands exploring her. His body, possessing hers...

"Alessia." Nicolo's voice was low. Rough. His eyes were hot as he watched her. "What are you thinking?"

Her heart was a swollen balloon, about to burst. She was

sure he knew precisely what she was thinking. All she had to do was whisper her answer.

You, she would say, as she had so many times the past days, and he would get down from his horse, hold up his arms and she would go into them and he would take her to the villa and even before their bedroom door closed, they'd be undressing each other, touching each other and perhaps this time, this time as he entered her he would say, *Alessia, my Alessia...*

"Principessa? Signore? Scusi, per favore...il principe—vostro padre—lui è qui!"

The maid who'd come after them was breathless with excitement. It was, evidently, one thing to deal with a princess—but a prince, *the* Prince Antoninni...

Alessia all but groaned. Her father was here. He would spoil her happiness. He would demand something, anything, and despite the fact that she was an adult, that she was here with her lover, she felt her heart start to plummet.

"Sweetheart?" She blinked. Nicolo stood beside the mare, arms raised, not to carry her to bed but to a confrontation with her father.

"Baby," he said softly, "come to me." And she all but tumbled into his outstretched arms.

Her safe haven, she thought in wonder. Her safe, warm haven against the world.

The visit didn't last long.

Nick wasn't very surprised. Though he had never before met the prince, he'd formed an opinion of him and it wasn't complimentary.

Antoninni's daughter was virtually living with a stranger. Yes, she was old enough to make her own choices. Still, if a man's daughter became involved with a stranger, wouldn't he want to have a conversation with that stranger, face-to-face?

Wouldn't he be interested in getting a feel for his daughter's lover?

Logically, the answer was "no." Nick couldn't recall ever meeting any of his mistress's fathers. Still, this was Italy. This was Tuscany. It was a place still caught in the cultural trappings of an earlier time.

And then there was the fact that Antoninni had gone to an acknowledged crime boss for a loan. That, the same as Alessia, he probably assumed that Nicolo, by virtue of being Cesare's son, was a thug, too.

Add it all up and that changed things, didn't it?

The simple answer was that it didn't.

Nick had expected…what? At the very worst, a demand as to what his intentions were. He had no answer to that but the question would have been valid. A father had the right to ask such a thing. At the very least, he'd figured on a thinly veiled warning that he was to treat Alessia as she deserved or there would be consequences.

Wrong on both counts, Nick thought as the prince's chauffeured limousine drove off.

The prince had greeted him with a handshake, Alessia with a cursory nod. He'd thanked Nick for the ten million euros that had been credited to his bank account, referring to it only obliquely, calling it "your investment."

Then he'd commented on a variety of things.

The weather. "I hope it will remain dry and pleasant throughout your visit, *Signore* Orsini."

The red Ferrari parked outside. "An excellent choice in automobiles, I must say. Though you must someday try a Lamborghini."

The villa. "A magnificent place, *Signore* Orsini!"

Done with small talk, he'd glanced at his watch, said he had another engagement and that he hoped to see Nick again before he left for New York. Another handshake, and Antoninni had turned to the door.

Nick, who'd stood all through the visit with his arm possessively curved around Alessia's waist, felt her stiffen.

"Father," she said. "How is Mother?"

The prince didn't bother looking back. "Your mother is fine," he said coolly.

Then he was gone.

Nick had grown up in a home in which conversations often didn't mean what they seemed to mean. Once they were alone, he turned Alessia toward him. The expression on her face damned near stopped his heart.

"Sweetheart? What is it?"

She shook her head.

"Tell me." Nick put his hand under her chin, gently raised her face so her eyes met his. "What did you mean when you asked him about your mother? Is she ill?"

Alessia hesitated. Could she tell him the truth? That her mother had lived most of the last two decades in an institution? She never talked of it to anyone, not out of shame or embarrassment but because of the way people reacted.

"Sweetheart?"

But this was not "anyone." This was Nicolo, and she took a deep, deep breath.

"My mother is in a hospital. A—a place for those who are—who are mentally ill."

Yes, this was Nicolo. Still, she prepared herself for what she thought of as the "oh, how awful" reaction, the elevated eyebrows of shock, the tsk-tsk of pity. It always made her feel not just helpless but angry.

It was the pity she could not stand.

"I'm sorry, baby," he said softly. "That must be rough."

Alessia looked at her lover. There was compassion in his

face and in his words. Not pity. Not disgust. She felt her heart lift.

"You must miss her terribly."

She nodded. "*Sì.* I do."

Nicolo drew her close in his arms. "What can I do to make things better, sweetheart? Would you like to visit her? I'll take you to wherever she is. If you let me, if she's up to it, I'd like to meet her."

That was the moment Alessia knew, without any doubt at all, that she had fallen in love, deeply in love, with the man whose arms enclosed her.

It was a two-hour drive to the sanitarium.

She couldn't believe Nicolo had offered to do it or that she'd accepted, she knew only that for the first time since her mother had been placed in the institution, walking through the doors and into the brightly lit, overly cheerful reception area didn't send tremors of anxiety through her. She never knew what to expect. Mama might be cheerful today; she might be despairing. She might not even acknowledge Alessia's presence, but no matter.

Alessia could face anything; Nicolo was with her.

As it turned out, her mother was at her best. She knew Alessia, smiled and offered Nicolo her hand when Alessia introduced him.

Nick raised her hand to his lips. "Now I know where your daughter gets her beauty, *principessa,*" he said with a smile.

They didn't stay long. Her mother's private duty nurse appeared and said it was time for her nap.

"Alessia," the princess said, "you must bring your handsome fiancé to see me again."

"Oh, no, Mama. Nicolo isn't—"

"I'll see to it that she does," Nick said, squeezing Alessia's hand.

So what if Alessia's mother believed he was engaged to her daughter? Nick thought as they drove back to the villa on the hilltop. From what Alessia had said, she probably wouldn't remember meeting him. Why not let her be happy, if only for today?

Besides, the real happiness would be that of the lucky guy who could someday truly make that claim.

Nick felt a strange constriction in his throat. He looked at his lover. Then he reached for her hand and wove his fingers through hers.

Time passed with startling speed.

Nick had previously phoned his PA, arranged for her to shift meetings and appointments. He'd lucked out with the Chicago deal—the banker he was to meet with had to cancel. The same with the Beijing appointment; the Chinese associate had called to ask if they could postpone their meeting for a few weeks.

On a sunny morning, he and Alessia drove to Florence. It turned out that what he'd packed in his carry-on was only enough to take him just so far.

"Man cannot live by one suit, jeans, running shorts and a tux alone," he'd intoned solemnly that morning, to the sweet sound of her laughter, and she, female to the marrow of her bones, had happily dragged him from shop to shop while he acquired new clothes.

It was her turn, he said after lunch. Over her protests, he stepped inside a shop that bore an elegant name and instructed the beaming sales clerk to outfit his lady from head to toe.

Alone while Alessia tried on dresses and trousers and anything and everything the clerk brought out for his approval, Nick took out his cell phone and did what he'd been putting off doing. He phoned his brothers, a three-way call,

Dante and Rafe and him, because Falco was still off on his honeymoon.

"Hey," Rafe said, "where the heck are you, man?"

"In Florence. I'm, ah, I'm on business for the old man."

He could almost see his brothers roll their eyes.

"Yeah," Dante said, "we figured he finally trapped you. How's it going?"

Alessia stepped onto the round platform in front of him and twirled in a circle. The blues, greens and violets of a very short, very strapless dress swirled around her thighs.

"Nick? How's it going?"

Nick cleared his throat. "Fine. Just fine."

"What's he got you doing, anyway?"

Alessia raised her eyebrows. Nick grinned, gave the dress a thumbs-up.

"Oh, this and that," he said casually. "You know."

In New York, sitting across from each other at a desk, Dante and Rafe looked meaningfully at each other.

Uh-oh, Dante mouthed, and Rafe nodded in agreement.

"Listen, man," Rafe said, "if we can help…"

Alessia was back again, this time in a short red dress that clung to every curve.

"Nick? I said, if we can help—"

"No," Nick said quickly. "No. Thanks, but I don't need any help. Really, things are going great. I just—I might not be home for a while."

Silence. Then Dante said, "Okay, let me be blunt. This thing the old man sent you to do… Does it involve some woman?"

"No," Nick said blithely.

"Because, the thing is, if it does—"

"Whoa. Sorry, guys. The call's breaking up," Nick said, and snapped shut the phone.

He hadn't lied, he told himself as the clerk showed him a

handful of silk thongs, not at all. Because this thing, for lack of a better phrase, this thing didn't involve "some" woman.

It involved one woman. Only one. And when that one woman came out of the dressing room, cheeks rosy with indignation, and told him that the clerk said that the gentleman was paying for everything, for each and every item she'd tried on, and that if he thought she would ever permit him to do that he was crazy—

"I *am* crazy," Nick said softly, gathering her into his arms. "Crazy for you."

Alessia held Nicolo's hand as they strolled across the *Ponte Vecchio,* the beautiful antique gold heart he'd just bought at a goldsmith's shop warm in the hollow of her throat.

She was happy. No. That was too small a word for what she felt. Her heart was full of joy. Of love.

Of what she had discovered about her lover.

That he was good and kind. Generous and compassionate. That he was perfect.

Of course she'd fallen in love with him. What woman wouldn't? What woman wouldn't want to be his forever—and yes, she knew she was thinking much, much too far ahead but how could she not imagine that he might love her, too? That he might ask her to be his wife, to bear his—to bear his—

Dio mio!

She could almost feel the blood drain from her head. Her footsteps faltered; she came to a dead stop, heart thumping so loudly she thought it might leap from her breast.

No, she told herself, no! It was impossible!

She should have had her period five days ago.

And she hadn't. She hadn't! And she was always, always regular....

"Princess?"

Alessia looked up at her lover. "I—I just realized..." Stop

it, she told herself furiously. Stay calm. Somehow, she managed to smile. "I have to stop at a pharmacy."

He said he would help her find one. She said she knew of a shop nearby. When he started to walk into the place with her, she stopped him.

"I must purchase something—something personal."

He flashed that devastating grin. Teased her. Said he was old enough not to be shocked at seeing a woman buy personal things. She knew he thought she meant she had to buy tampons. *Dio, if only that were so!*

Somehow, she made herself smile in return.

"This is Italy," she said in a teasing tone. "You might not be shocked, *signore,* but others would be."

It was a lie, but he could not know it. He rolled his eyes, said okay, he'd wait outside, and then he hauled her to her toes and kissed her on her mouth and she wanted to clutch his shoulders and tell him that she was terrified.

Instead, she went into the pharmacy and bought half a dozen early pregnancy test kits.

At the villa, she told him she needed privacy to try on the things he'd bought her and choose one outfit for dinner on the terrace. He kissed her again, said she could make him a supremely happy man if she let him watch and she clucked her tongue, told him to go away and he rolled his eyes again, kissed her...

Finally, Alessia was alone.

Her hands shook as she opened the kits.

She took the tests, one after another, drinking as much water as she could between them, but the results were all the same.

She was pregnant. Pregnant! How could it have happened?

She was on the pill. She'd been on it for almost a year, ever since her gynecologist had told her it might help ease the crippling pain she suffered every month. Nicolo had asked her if she used birth control, and even though it wasn't birth control, not for her, she'd assured him that she was....

Alessia stared at herself in the mirror, hands braced for support on the bathroom sink as the world began to turn gray.

But she had not been. Not that night. She always took her pill at bedtime but she had not taken it that night; she had left the little packet in her room at her father's villa and in the excitement of making love, such incredible love with Nicolo, she had forgotten everything but him.

When had she finally taken another pill?

She sank to the cool marble floor. A sob rose in her throat. She put her hand to her lips, bit down on her thumb to muffle the sound.

Not until two days—and two nights—later, when they'd returned to Villa Antoninni so they could retrieve their things.

She had missed three of the pills. Three! How could she have been so stupid? She had messed up and now she was pregnant. Nicolo's baby was in her womb, tiny and helpless.

And unplanned. Unplanned and surely unwanted by its father...

"Alessia? Sweetheart, I've been waiting downstairs for you. Are you okay?"

Her heart pounded. She shot to her feet and swept all the EPT boxes and sticks into the wastebasket.

"Alessia. Answer me. Are you ill?"

"No," she said in a high voice that bore no resemblance to her own. "I mean, yes, *sì*, I am. I—I have my period and—and—"

"Baby. Open the door."

"No! Nicolo, *per favore,* I told you, this is a female thing."

Nick narrowed his eyes. He knew about "female things."

When you grew up in a house with two sisters, the mystery wasn't all that mysterious. His sister Isabella waltzed through her monthly cycle. Anna, on the other hand, crept around clutching a heating pad to her belly.

But he'd never heard Anna or any other woman sobbing and, dammit, Alessia had been sobbing.

Female thing or not, no way was his princess going to endure any kind of pain without him doing whatever he could to help.

"I'm coming in," he said in a tone that said he wasn't going to tolerate any nonsense.

"No, Nicolo—"

Nick swung the door open. Alessia was sitting on the edge of the marble tub, eyes red and swollen, face shiny with tears.

His heart melted.

"Ah, sweetheart…"

"Nicolo," she said brokenly, and went straight into his arms.

Nick swept her off her feet and carried her into the bedroom. He sat down in a velvet armchair, drew her head against his chest and crooned to her, rocked her gently as he held her close. Long moments went by. Her sobs eased; her tears stopped. He waited a few seconds. Then he drew back and looked at her tearstained face. This was more than pain from her period. Every instinct told him so.

"Princess." Gently, he smoothed her hair back from her damp cheeks. "What is it?"

Alessia looked at Nicolo. His eyes were filled with concern. His arms were a bulwark against the woes of the world. He was a good, kind man. He had not signed on for this.

She could lie to him. Tell him she wept because her period was agony. Tell him almost anything. He would believe her, if she told the lie well enough.

"Alessia. Talk to me." He took her hands, brought them to his lips. "Tell me why you're crying."

It was just as the poets said. Time did stand still. She took a steadying breath.

"Nicolo," she whispered, "Nicolo—I am pregnant."

CHAPTER TWELVE

PREGNANT.

The word echoed in Nick's head. Alessia was pregnant.

He felt a sheen of cold sweat break out on his forehead. If there was one word a man never wanted to hear from a woman with whom he was having an affair, that was it.

Over the years, he'd grown accustomed to hearing women say things that were upsetting. Like *I love you.* Like *I know you said you weren't interested in a serious relationship but...* And on one memorable occasion, *But what will my friends say if we break up?*

Women said those things in different ways, never mind that he always made it clear, right up front, he wasn't looking for forever. For all he knew, "forever" didn't really exist.

So, yes, he'd heard women say a lot of things but he'd never had one claim she was...

"Pregnant?" The word came out sounding rusty. Nick cleared his throat. "Are you certain?"

"Sì."

"How do you know?"

"I took a test. Many tests." Her hands, still enclosed by his, were trembling. "That was what I was doing in the bathroom."

"Have you missed your period?"

She blushed. And wasn't that ridiculous? he thought, as

coldness seeped into his blood. Her body had no secrets from him, not anymore, and she was telling him she was knocked up…but asking her about her menstrual cycle made her blush.

"I should have had it last week. I—I did not realize that it had not—"

Carefully, he let go of her hands. "You said you were on the pill."

"I was. I am." Her eyes met his. "But I did not have my pills with me that first night, Nicolo, and we made—we made love so many times before we went back to my father's villa and I collected my things…"

"So, you weren't on the pill. Not really, even though you said you were."

She winced. Okay. He knew the question was coldly phrased, maybe even unfairly phrased but, dammit, she had said—

Nick eased Alessia off his lap, got to his feet and paced across the room before swinging around to face her.

"How could this have happened?"

She felt everything within her collapse. She knew his real question was, how could she have let this happen? It didn't surprise her. In a world that talked about the equality of women, nothing was equal when it came to sex. She had always known that. At university, men who had a lot of lovers were sexy; women who took equal numbers of men were sluts.

As for getting pregnant outside of wedlock… Perhaps it was fine for Hollywood movie stars but it was far from fine in her world. Getting pregnant when you shouldn't was invariably the woman's fault, just as it was the woman's responsibility to deal with.

Nicolo had not said any of those things. He didn't have to. The way he felt was in his tone, his face, the very tension radiating from him.

"I told you," she said, trying to stay calm. "I forgot—"

"Are you sure," he said, his tone as brutal as it was flat, "are you absolutely sure I'm the man who made you pregnant?"

She had expected the question. Still, she hated him for asking it. She wanted to scream. To hurl herself at him and beat her fists against his chest.

How could he even think he was not the man whose seed had joined with her egg?

And yet—and yet, she thought on a dizzying rush of despair, she knew how he could think it.

She had gone into his arms after knowing him for a couple of hours, slept with him a day later. She had given herself to him fully, nothing held back. She had done things with him she had never imagined she would ever do.

But he could know nothing of that.

She knew he'd had many women; a man like him would. He moved in a world where people tumbled into bed casually, without regrets. She didn't—or maybe it was more truthful to say such things *did* happen in her world.

But not to her.

He couldn't possibly know that her friends teased her about her pathetic sex life. He couldn't know she hadn't been with a man in almost four years. So, no, she couldn't blame him for asking if the life growing within her womb was his.

She could blame only herself for being foolish enough to have thought, even fleetingly, that what they'd found was not just sex but love.

"I asked you a question. Are you sure I'm the man who—"

Alessia's despair gave way to anger. It was a safer emotion. How dare he accuse her of lying about such a thing or, at the very least, of having gone from someone else's arms to his?

"No," she said coldly, "no, I'm not. It might have been the butcher. Or the man from the cleaning service. And then there's the concierge at my apartment building in Rome and the headwaiter at a restaurant where I had dinner last week, and if not him, the drummer from a punk rock band whose publicity I have handled or—"

Nicolo covered the distance between them in four strides and grasped her by the shoulders.

"You think this is funny?"

"I think I was stupid even to tell you about this." Her eyes flashed fire. "Forget that I said anything, *signore*. This is not your problem, it is mine."

"Hey. I never said—"

"I am accustomed to taking care of myself. I do not require your help or anyone else's." Angrily, she shrugged free of his hands. "I would not have told you anything if you had not intruded on my privacy."

His dark eyebrows rose. "Excuse me?"

"The bathroom door was closed. I asked you not to open it but you did. And you found me at the worst possible moment. I was—I was surprised by what I had just learned." It was the understatement of the century, but he didn't have to know that. Alessia lifted her chin. "So, if you had not intruded—"

Nick cursed. His hands bit into her flesh as he hoisted her to her toes.

"That's rubbish and you damned well know it!" he said, his voice rough with anger. "You're pregnant. I got you that way. That makes this my problem as much as yours."

His words should have warmed her. They didn't. The pregnancy was, indeed, a problem—but she didn't like hearing him call it that. Stupid, she knew, but that was how she felt. Her mother had been her father's "problem" all his life, or so he claimed. There wasn't a way in the world she was going to be seen as a "problem" by Nicolo Orsini or any other man.

"Let go of me," she said with icy calm.

"Don't talk to me about intruding on your privacy, not when

that so-called 'privacy' involves something that's bound to change both our lives forever."

"I do not take orders from you, Mr. Orsini!"

Sweet Mary, Nick thought, what kind of nonsense was this?

First, she dropped a bomb of nuclear proportions in his lap. Then she all but told him what he could do with his help. Okay, maybe he'd left something out, the part where he'd demanded to know how in hell this could have happened and was she sure the kid was his—if you could call a two-week-old clump of cells a kid—but, dammit, what man wouldn't ask?

The lady had more attitude than any woman he'd ever known. It made him want to shake some sense into her...or maybe kiss some sense into her. One or the other and it didn't much matter which because sense was what she needed.

Did she think he'd walk away from what was as much his responsibility as hers? Yes, she'd said she was on the pill. So what? He was always a responsible lover. He should have used a condom. He always did.

Except with her.

Hell.

Nick let go of Alessia, swung around and took a long breath. Who was he kidding? Not taking her that night would have been impossible. He would have died unless he could have undressed her, kissed her, buried himself deep inside her...

Merda!

Sex was the last thing he should be thinking about right now. He'd got himself into a mess. Now, he had to find a way out and yeah, he had to find a way out of it for her, too. What was that old saying? It took two to tango.

And it sure took two to make a baby.

Well, then. It took two to deal with whatever came next. She might not like it, might consider his input another intrusion, for God's sake, but she'd have to accept it. He wasn't going to let her do otherwise.

"Okay," he said, doing his best to sound calm. "Okay, what we need to do is discuss this calmly. Very calmly, because—"

He turned toward her and his heart damned near stopped.

For all that imperious air, that "do not touch me" coldness he'd seen in her when they'd first met, what he saw now was the woman he'd come to—to care about. Care about? Even now, his muscles taut, his mind racing like a hamster on a wheel…even now, he wanted her, wanted her as he had never in his life imagined wanting a woman.

Her expression was defiant but her eyes were filled with fear. She was trembling even though the room was warm and he thought of how easily he could stop those tremors, stay her tears by taking her in his arms and kissing her, kissing her until she clung to him.

A groan of despair caught in his throat as he walked past her, out the door and out of the villa.

Hands in his pockets, head down, Nick climbed the hill behind the house. The sun was setting; shadows had accumulated in the olive grove, turning the trees into otherworldly creatures with long, lean bodies and spindly arms. The hoot of an owl added to the seeming strangeness of the landscape and to the confusion in his soul.

No way could he go on blaming this on Alessia. He was as responsible as she, maybe even more. He'd seen to it that she'd forgotten everything the night he'd brought her here, not just the birth control pills but the world outside.

He was the one who'd planned everything.

Planned? Nick barked out a laugh.

Some planner he'd turned out to be. A house. A bed. His

stupid brain hadn't gone beyond the necessities. And a supply of condoms should have been part of those necessities. He'd known that since he was, what, thirteen, sitting through the embarrassment of a sex-ed class, then snickering over what it all meant a couple of hours later with his brothers.

He kicked at a small stone, watched it tumble downhill.

The simple truth was that sex had been the only thing on his mind. Having Alessia. Making love with her. Making her his, as if sleeping with a woman marked her as a man's property.

A man didn't make a woman "his" unless he married her. And marriage was a million light-years away.

You could double those light-years when it came to having kids. Kids were not part of the plan. The best he'd concede was that maybe someday he'd want them, but for now...

No kids.

They weren't in Alessia's plans, either. Not from what he'd seen when he'd opened that bathroom door. Her tears. Her disbelief. No, clearly she wasn't in the market for motherhood.

She was young. Beautiful. So damned beautiful, with the world waiting for her to explore it.

Calmer now, he knew that whatever she decided to do—terminate the pregnancy, go through with it and keep the baby, go through with it and give the baby up for adoption—her world would never be the same again.

And it was his fault.

Nick stopped walking, tucked his hands in his pockets and gazed up at the sky. Night was coming on quickly. A handful of stars flamed against the dark blue canopy; a fat yellow moon was rising on the horizon.

Amazing.

The world changed but life went on. And, yes, his world had changed. No matter what choice Alessia made, he'd always know he'd been the reason she'd had to make that choice. He'd always know that he'd created a life that had ended before it began. Or that strangers were raising a kid with his genes, his DNA. And even if Alessia decided to keep the child, it would not have a father.

Yes, of course, he'd acknowledge the kid and support it. Maybe he'd even visit. Or maybe not. Maybe she wouldn't want his daughter to have only sporadic contact with the man who was her father in only the most scientific terms. His son or his daughter, yes, but somehow it was easier to picture a little girl with Alessia's features, her golden hair, her blue eyes...

What was that?

A car was coming up the long drive that led to the villa. A car, at this time of evening? Why should a car...

It was a taxi. It had to be. Who but a cabby would stop outside the house and blast his horn like that? It was the loud, impolite, "I'm here—where are you?" language of cab drivers everywhere.

A taxi.

Nick cursed and raced for the villa. "Dammit," he said as he ran, "dammit to hell, Alessia..."

The front door opened just as he reached it. And yeah, there she was, overnight bag in hand.

She was leaving him. *Leaving him!* How dare she? Did she really think she could take a step like that without first asking him if he'd let her go?

He stood at the foot of the steps, fists planted on his hips, eyes hot with anger.

"Where in hell do you think you're going?"

Alessia narrowed her eyes, gave him the same sort of princess-to-peasant look she had at the airport a million years ago.

"Get out of my way, please."

Please? He snorted. The "please" might as well have been a four-letter word.

"*Signore* Orsini. I asked you to—"

The taxi horn blasted. Nick shot the cabby a furious look, then turned back to Alessia.

"You are not to move," he growled.

She laughed. Laughed, damn her, and came down the steps. He caught her arm, leaned down, his face an inch from hers.

"I'm warning you, princess. Do not take another step."

"Who are you to give me orders?"

"I'll tell you exactly who I am. I am Nicolo Orsini. And unless you want to find out what that means, you will not, under any circumstances, move from this spot. *Capisce?*"

"How dare you give me orders? I am a princess. I am descended from kings. And you—you—"

Nick kissed her. Hard. Deep. He forced her head back and she gasped and struck him with her free hand and he caught that hand, brought it behind her back and went on kissing her until she moaned into his mouth and her lips parted to the possessive thrust of his tongue.

Then he let her go.

She stood motionless as he trotted down the steps, dug out his wallet and stuffed a handful of bills into the cabby's extended hand. The taxi roared away. Nick stood still for a couple of seconds before he returned to confront Alessia.

"Where," he said grimly, "did you think you were going?"

"It's none of your—"

"You tell me you're having my baby. Then you turn tail and run."

She drew herself up. "What is this 'turning tail' thing?"

"It means you were afraid to stay and face me."

"I am not afraid of you. I was—I was simply going away."

Nick folded his arms. "I'll ask you again. Where were you going?"

Where, indeed? Alessia swallowed hard.

"Away."

"You're going to have to do better than that."

"You do not have the right to—"

Nick clasped her shoulders again, his touch harsh.

"I have every right! Where were you going? What are your plans?" His mouth twisted. "Dammit, that's my child you're carrying."

Her eyes flashed with bitterness. "Are you sure?"

Okay. He deserved that. Nick took a deep breath.

"Just give me a straight answer. What are you going to do about the baby?" His eyes met hers; he could feel his anger draining away. "Listen. This isn't easy for me, either. Talk to me. Tell me what you're thinking, what you want to do."

She went on glaring at him. Then, suddenly, the fight seemed to go out of her and she slumped in his hands.

"I don't—I don't know." She looked up at him, eyes pleading for understanding. "Do you think I can decide something like this in an hour? In a day? My life has changed, Nicolo. Whatever I do, nothing will ever be the same again."

It was exactly what he'd been thinking in the olive grove. Everything had changed for him, for her. Forever. And, just that quickly, his anger was gone.

"Come here," he said softly, gathering her to him. She fought him, but only for a second. Then she gave a little hiccup of a sob. His arms closed tightly around her; she laid her head against his chest.

"You're right," he said, one big hand gently stroking her hair. "Nothing will ever be the same again for either of us. We have a decision to make, princess, maybe the most important decision of our lives."

Alessia shut her eyes. Nicolo's touch was so soothing. She longed to wind her arms around his neck, let herself lean into him, let his strength seep into her.

She didn't. She couldn't. This was a time for rational thought, not for dreams. And letting herself fall in love with this man had been a dream.

He was not hers. He never would be. But it was a comfort to know she had not been wrong about him. He was a good man. A kind man. That he had refused to let her leave, that he spoke of the decision that came next as having to be made by them both, even that he was holding her now with such tenderness, proved it.

But it didn't change the fact that their relationship was over. What else could it be?

"Alessia. Come inside. We'll sit down, have some coffee, talk about this." He tipped her face to his. "We can work this through, sweetheart. You'll see."

She let him hold her hand and lead her into the villa, take her straight through it to the terrace at the back and out into the warm night. How fitting that they should come outside to discuss what would happen next. She'd sat outdoors on a warm Tuscan evening a few short weeks ago with her father. It was where she had first heard the name Orsini.

Who could have imagined that Nicolo Orsini would become her lover? Who could have imagined his child would lie sleeping in her womb?

Nicolo led her to a love seat, drew her down next to him, held her hands so that they faced each other.

"So," he said softly.

She couldn't help offering a little smile.

"So," she said.

Nicolo freed one of his hands, used it to tuck a strand of hair behind her ear.

"Tell me what you're thinking. About what you want to do next."

She took a deep breath. "There are public clinics. Private doctors. Abortion is legal in my country."

"But?"

"But, it is not a good choice for me."

"You want to have the baby."

She nodded.

"And then what?"

Alessia caught her bottom lip between her teeth. This part wasn't as clear yet. She was a career woman. Was it right to bring a child into a life like hers? To raise it without a father? Or was it better to give it up for adoption?

There were plenty of couples who were eager for a child—but could she do that without wondering about her baby for the rest of her life? Was he happy? Was he well? And yes, already, she thought of the baby inside her as "he," a little boy with Nicolo's features. His dark hair. His beautiful eyes.

"And then what?" Nicolo said again, his voice a low rumble. "After the baby's born…what do you want to do with her?"

"With him," she said, without thinking.

Nicolo smiled. "With him. What next, princess?"

Alessia took a deep breath. The answer had been there all along. She just hadn't seen it clearly until now.

"I'll keep my baby."

"Good," Nicolo said, gathering her against him. "That's what I hoped you'd say."

Ah. Now his questions made sense. He was going to offer to support the child. She didn't want that. A clean break was best. She would work hard, earn enough money to give her baby everything he needed.…

"It's good," he said, "because that's what I want, too." He

cupped her shoulders, held her at arm's length and looked into her eyes. "Alessia. Will you marry me?"

Her mouth dropped open. It made Nick want to laugh. Or kiss her and that, he decided, was the far better choice. Slowly, he bent to her, brought his lips to hers.

"Marry me, princess," he whispered. "And we'll raise our baby together."

Alessia stared at him. "Marry you? No. It's a wonderful gesture, Nicolo, but—"

"We owe this child more than a gesture."

"I know. I mean, I understand that. But marriage…"

"Is it such a horrible thought? Marrying me? Becoming Mrs. Nicolo Orsini?"

Horrible? She fought to keep from saying the words singing in her blood, that she loved him, adored him, that spending her life with him would be the dream she'd been afraid to dream.

"Princess?"

He was waiting for her answer. She wanted to say "yes," but could she marry a man who didn't love her, no matter how noble the reason?

"What?" he said. "What are you thinking?"

Alessia touched the tip of her tongue to her dry lips.

"I'm thinking…I'm thinking, what about love?"

Nick captured Alessia's lips with his. He kissed her again and again and when he raised his head, her eyes were glazed, her lips rosy and swollen.

"What about it?" he said gruffly.

What, indeed? she thought.

And then he began undressing her and she stopped thinking about anything but him.

CHAPTER THIRTEEN

THEY would have a civil ceremony.

It was the fastest way to marry. Even so, Alessia said, they would have to wait two weeks.

"Tomorrow," Nick said the next morning, as they lay in their rumpled bed.

Alessia laughed. "Impossible."

"Because?"

"Because, this is *Italia*. There are laws to obey. Are there not laws in America?"

"We're not in America," he said, brushing his lips over hers. "We're in *Italia,* just as you said. And I am an impatient man."

"Well, *signore impaziente,* there is nothing you can do about it. The law is the law."

"And you know the law, princess?"

"I do," she said archly.

She was in public relations. She had made marriage arrangements for others. Nicolo, as an American citizen, could marry simply by filing the necessary papers. But it was different for an Italian national. For her. Banns would have to be posted for two Sundays prior to the day of the ceremony.

Nick rolled her beneath him.

"We'll see about that," he said.

"Nicolo. There is nothing to see. The law is the law."

She sounded like a schoolteacher correcting a recalcitrant pupil. It made him smile. He loved her all-knowing tone, loved the slightly exasperated look on her face. He loved—he loved...

"What are you thinking?" Alessia said softly.

"Let me show you," he said huskily, and he ended all further discussion the best possible way, with kisses, with his mouth on her breasts, with his body hard and demanding inside hers.

As he had done to find their villa, Nick made a couple of phone calls.

In midafternoon, a messenger came to the door with a manila envelope. Nick opened it, checked the contents and grinned.

"What?" Alessia said.

His grin widened. "Time to shop for a wedding dress, princess."

Her breath caught. "You mean..." She nodded at the open envelope and the papers spilling out of it. "Is that about the banns?"

"What banns?" Nicolo said and kissed her.

He took her into the heart of Florence, to a boutique he'd noticed one evening as they'd strolled the street after dinner at a small café.

"We want a dress," he told the clerk.

The woman looked from Nick to Alessia, then at him again. "Is it for a special occasion?"

"Very special," Nick said solemnly. His arm tightened around Alessia's waist. "We're getting married tomorrow."

Nick smiled. Alessia blushed. The clerk grinned. An hour later, they left the shop with a pale pink silk dress and matching jacket, a tiny gold purse and gold stilettos.

It was dusk, and the temperature had dropped. Perhaps that was why Alessia shuddered.

"Cold, sweetheart?"

She nodded and Nicolo drew her closer as they made their way to the Ferrari but the truth was, Alessia wasn't really cold. She'd shuddered because a thought had crept into her mind. Things were moving so fast. Was Nicolo hurrying the arrangements because he didn't want to give her time her to change her mind? Or was it because he didn't want to give *himself* time to change *his* mind?

She shuddered again, because she didn't want to think about it.

Nick knew he was rushing things, but he had a good reason.

Any delay and his family might somehow learn what was happening. The Orsinis, especially his brothers, were good at uncovering secrets. And if they uncovered this one, the wedding would become a circus.

His mother and his sisters would shriek with female delight and go straight into action. He'd seen it happen with Rafe, Dante and Falco. The church. The music. The reception. The cake. The menu. The flowers. The gowns. The tuxes.

And his brothers. They'd go straight for the jugular. *You know her two weeks? What, did you knock her up?* Well, yeah, he had. But as well-meaning as the question would be, he'd have to answer with his fists because this was Alessia and whether she was pregnant or not wasn't their concern. She was going to be his wife, and his decision wasn't up for a vote.

Besides, the more he thought about it, the more certain he felt that he was doing the right thing. His baby—the baby he and Alessia had created—deserved a father.

And the woman he was marrying was a joy. She was beautiful. Bright. She could make him laugh. She could make him feel a tenderness he'd never known he possessed. The marriage was sudden, yes. But it would work out. It would be successful.

In fact, after the initial shock of trying to visualize himself as a married man, the idea had become, well, it had become kind of pleasant. He liked the idea of greeting the day with Alessia in his arms and ending it the same way.

Marriages had been built on less.

Still, this one needed a little time, a little space. Bottom line? The wedding first, followed by a honeymoon. After that, he'd contact his brothers, break the news, ask them to tell his mother and sisters. When all that was done, he'd take Alessia to New York to meet his family.

Right now, the only person he had to inform was her father. The prince probably knew everyone in Florence; he'd surely hear the news and Nick wanted it to come from him, not secondhand.

He disliked Antoninni. He'd run a centuries-old vineyard to the point of ruin. Far worse, he'd left his daughter alone to deal with Cesare Orsini, and he seemed to have little affection for her.

But he was Alessia's father.

That night, while she prepared for bed, Nick phoned him, reached his voice mail and left a brief message.

"This is Nicolo Orsini. Your daughter has done me the honor of agreeing to become my wife. The wedding is tomorrow, ten in the morning, in the *Sala Rossa* of the *Palazzo Vecchio*. You are, of course, welcome to attend."

It was not a warm message but it was the right one.

And Nick, in fact all the Orsini brothers, had always been big on doing that which was right.

The next day dawned bright and sunny.

A few minutes before ten, Alessia clung tightly to Nicolo's hand as they walked into the palazzo.

Nicolo had reassured her as she lay in his arms. "This will be a good marriage," he'd said softly.

She wanted to believe him, but she was marrying him for love—and he was marrying her only because he was a responsible, decent man.

He was the opposite of her father.... And suddenly, she realized she had no idea if her father had kept the promise he'd made about her mother's care. Had he? Was Mama still safely in the sanitarium she had come to think of as home?

The mayor, who would perform the ceremony, was strolling toward them with her father a few steps behind. Alessia turned to Nicolo, put her hand lightly on his arm.

"The mayor will surely want to speak with you," she said quickly. "While he does that, I must talk to my father."

Nicolo put his hand over hers. "Can it wait until after the ceremony, sweetheart?"

Her heart felt as if it were going to overflow at the tenderness in his voice.

"This is important, Nicolo. I only need a moment, *sì?*"

Her bridegroom tipped her face to his and brushed his lips over hers.

"You don't need my permission, princess. A last private word between father and daughter? Sure. Go ahead." He smiled. "Just remember to get back here in time to become my wife."

She smiled, rose on her toes to kiss his cheek. Then she hurried to the prince and motioned toward an alcove.

The prince's smile was sly.

"Congratulations, daughter. What a coup! The wife of an Orsini. *Eccellente!*"

Alessia ignored the comment. "Tell me about my mother," she said in a low voice.

"Tell you what? She is fine."

"Have you kept her at the sanitarium, as you promised? We

had an agreement. I would be your hostess, take your place entertaining Cesare Orsini, and you—"

"And I would repay you for your actions." Antoninni smiled. "And what a hostess you were, Alessia!" He chuckled. "I knew you would do far better with the man than I ever could!"

"You mean, you always intended to have me step in?"

"Of course. Once Orsini told me he would send his son instead of coming to Florence himself…" The prince laughed softly. "Do not look so shocked, Alessia. You did a fine job. You not only secured my loan, you doubled it."

"It was Nicolo, not me. He is the one who decided to give you ten million euros."

"Ten million euros, and now I am to have one of New York's wealthiest, most powerful men as my son-in-law." Antoninni arched one eyebrow. "Are you carrying his child? Is that the reason for this swift marriage?"

"None of that concerns you," Alessia said sharply. "Our understanding was about my mother. Have you kept your word?"

A dramatic sigh. "I will."

Would he? Alessia doubted it. He'd pay for her mother's care for a while. Then he'd stop. She did a quick mental calculation of what it cost to care for her mother, what it might cost over the next years, and then she looked her father in the eye.

"You will deposit three million euros to my account immediately."

"Three mill— You joke, daughter. That is too much, even for your role in securing ten million euros, marriage to an Orsini and becoming pregnant with his—"

"Go on," Nicolo said coldly. "Let's hear the rest."

Alessia and her father spun around. Her father paled.

"*Signore* Orsini! I did not see you standing—"

"No. Obviously, you did not."

Alessia blanched. Nicolo had overheard...and, all at once, she was glad that he had. Why hadn't she shared her concerns with her lover sooner? There was nothing she couldn't tell him, not even when it was humiliating. Her father was a cold, unfeeling man; Nicolo was just the opposite. She could trust him to see to it that her father did as he had promised.

She could trust him with everything, for the rest of her life.

"Nicolo." She smiled tremulously. "I am glad you overheard our conversation. I should have told you that my father and I had an agreement—"

"I heard."

His voice was frigid, his eyes black as coal. He looked cruel and hard and dangerous, and she couldn't understand the reason.... Until, with terrible suddenness, she realized how easily he might have misconstrued her father's words, and hers.

"No! Oh, no, you don't understand—"

She gasped as his hand closed painfully around her wrist.

"I understand everything, *principessa*." His gaze dropped to her belly, then rose to her face. "Especially your touching story about being on the pill."

Her face went white. "You're wrong! I swear it, you are—"

"Say goodbye to Daddy, sweetheart. You won't be seeing him for a long time."

"Nicolo, Nicolo, *per favore*—"

"Don't look so stricken, baby." Nick's mouth twisted. "You still won the prize. I'm going to marry you. Hell, you're carrying my child. If you think I'd leave him to the tender mercies of you and Papa, you can think again."

"Nicolo." Alessia's voice trembled. "I know what you think you heard, but—"

"Get out of my sight," Nick told Antoninni. The prince, eyes wide with shock, took a step back. "If I ever see you again, so help me, I'll do what your kind has feared for the past six hundred years and use you to wipe the floor."

Antoninni scurried away like a rat. Alessia reached out her hand to Nicolo. She had never seen him like this, so furious, so vengeful, so cold. It terrified her.

"Nicolo, please, listen to—"

"I'm done listening, princess. We're here so you can finalize the deal you made with Daddy by becoming my wife."

"No! I never made such a deal!"

"Sorry. I should have said, we're here so you can improve the deal by becoming my wife."

"Oh, *Dio,* oh, God, please—"

"I'll pull the loan money," Nick said softly. "And then I'll use every ounce of that Orsini power you find so disgusting and I promise, I'll take my child away from you. What happens to you then, *principessa?*"

Alessia stared at him in horror. A muscle ticked in his jaw. He waited. Then, he held out his hand. Slowly, she put hers into it and he led her across the room, to where the mayor was waiting.

"No," Alessia said in a desperate whisper, "no, not like this!"

"Exactly like this," Nick said.

Five minutes later, they were man and wife.

He had planned to surprise his bride.

A honeymoon in Venice, at the Gritti Palace. Five days in a suite the concierge had assured him was as romantic as a newly married couple could wish, then a two-day stop in Milan so he could buy his bride a new wardrobe, and, finally a flight to New York in a chartered plane, a bottle of rare Krug Brut Multi-Vintage Rosé waiting in a silver bucket in the craft's private bedroom, the room itself filled with orchids and roses.

There would be none of that now.

Nick made quick adjustments to his plans. A stop at the villa outside Florence to pick up his things. A phone call to the charter service so he could change the arrangements he'd made, a drive to the airport where a plane awaited them without champagne or flowers.

But it had a private bedroom, he thought coldly as he kept a hard hand on his wife's elbow and climbed the steps into the cabin, because no way was he giving up the one thing Alessia Antoninni Orsini could provide him…until, of course, she delivered his child.

After that, after his son or daughter was born, he'd decide if he wanted his wife in his bed anymore or if her usefulness to him was at an end.

"Nicolo," Alessia said now, as the door to the plane slid shut behind them, "Nicolo, if you would only listen—"

It was what she'd been saying ever since he'd stumbled into what he'd stupidly assumed was a last conversation between a father before he gave his daughter into the care of the man who was now her husband. And, as he had done each time she'd asked him to listen, Nick ignored her.

Listen to what? More lies? He'd heard enough from that soft, sweet-tasting mouth to last a lifetime.

That she was sexually inexperienced.

That she had "forgotten" to take her birth control pills.

That he was her lover. Of it all, those two whispered words, *mio amante,* infuriated him the most. He'd known she hadn't meant it, that she'd said it in a haze of sexual heat. Hell, who cared what she'd called him? Still, honesty demanded he admit the truth to himself. All he was to her, all he'd ever been, was a ticket to a fat bank account.

He'd let her make a fool of him, he thought grimly as he drew her down next to him in a leather seat. He hated himself for having let even a part of his heart feel the impact of her sighs, her whispers, her caresses.

Sex, Nicolo thought coldly. That was all it had been. For him. For her. And he had every intention of making the most of it.

The plane's jet engines came to life. The aircraft moved slowly forward. And his lying, deceitful wife leaned toward him. "Nicolo," she said in a frantic whisper, "please…"

Nick shot to his feet, grasped her wrist and brought her up beside him. He walked purposefully toward the rear of the cabin, slid open the bedroom door and pushed her inside.

Then he shut the door and locked it.

"Take off your clothes," he growled.

She stared at him. Her eyes glittered, pools of darkest blue in her pale face.

"No. Nicolo—"

"Take them off. Or I'll do it for you."

Tears spilled down her cheeks. "You are not this kind of man," she whispered. "You are good. You are kind. You are—"

"I am Nick Orsini." His hands went to his jacket. Undid the buttons. He shrugged it off, unbuttoned his shirt, shrugged that off, too. "As far as you're concerned, I am exactly the man you expected me to be. I see what I want and I take it." A cruel smile twisted across his lips. "We suit each other, *principessa*. A man who takes what he wants. A woman who does the same."

He closed the distance between them, put his hand in the V of the pale pink silk dress that, only hours before, he had thought the most perfect thing a bride could wear. One hard tug, one gasp from her, and the dress tore and fell to her feet.

"Oh, God," she said, weeping, "Nicolo, don't—"

"I told you," he said grimly. "The name is Nick."

And he swept his wife into his arms and took her to bed.

He'd meant to take her coldly.

Pin her arms above her head if she fought him. Thrust his knee between her thighs. Take her hard, ride her hard, get himself off without giving a damn if she was ready or not.

Except, she didn't fight him.

She lay still, her face turned away from him. And she wept. Silently. Agonizingly. Her tears soaked the linen pillowcase; her teeth caught and held her bottom lip.

All his rage drained away. In its place was despair so terrible, so deep, that Nick felt his throat constrict.

He got to his feet. Put on his shirt. Tossed his jacket on a chair. She could use it to hide what he had done to her dress.

Then he walked out of the cabin, went to the front of the plane and sank into a seat.

And knew that he had touched his wife, his achingly beautiful, heartbreakingly dishonest wife, for the very last time.

CHAPTER FOURTEEN

THE marriage had been a mistake.

Nick sat in his leather swivel chair, his back to a massive oak desk, staring out his office windows at the narrow streets of Soho four stories below. He'd endured another day of meetings and phone calls just as he'd done for the past couple of weeks by deliberately blanking his mind to anything but business.

Now, in the waning hours of the long day, he had the one thing he didn't want.

Time to think.

It was the same every day. Work kept him busy. Busier than ever. He'd taken on meetings and calls that should have been his brothers' responsibilities. They were happy to let him do it. Things were happening in their lives. Rafe and Chiara were eagerly preparing for the arrival of their first child. Dante and Gabriella had their hands full with their cute toddler. Falco and Elle were looking for a weekend home in Connecticut.

"You sure you don't mind?" they'd say, when he offered to take a meeting in their place.

"Hey," he'd say lightly, "what are brothers for?" Or he'd flash a smile and say he'd get even some day and payback would be hell.

What he didn't say, had not said, had no intention of saying, was that he was as married as they were. His marriage, his wife, the child she carried...

Secrets, known only to him.

There was no way he could keep secrets like those from his family forever.

"Dammit," he said wearily.

Nick turned toward his desk, propped his elbows on its paper-strewn surface and put his face in his hands.

He wasn't as married as his brothers. He knew damned well that neither Rafe or Dante or Falco went home to silence at the end of the day, or to a meal eaten alone, or that any of them slept alone as he did, while his wife slept in a bedroom at the end of the hall. And he'd have bet everything that he was the only one who cursed himself a dozen times a day for having been used and trapped into marriage because he'd let himself be played for a fool.

Nick sat back and dragged air deep into his lungs.

Most of all, he was damned sure that none of his brothers lay awake at night, staring into the darkness and fighting the almost overpowering need to say to hell with all this, go to his wife's room, fling open the door or break the freaking thing down if he had to, strip away the duvet that covered her and take her again and again even if she begged him not to do it, take her mercilessly until he'd worked her out of his system forever.

Or until she sobbed his name, wound her arms around his neck and told him that he was her lover, that he was more than that, that he was her love....

"Merda!"

Nick shot to his feet, jammed his hands into his pockets and paced the big room.

What he needed was sex. Not with his wife. Sex with a woman who would respond to him with honesty rather than calculated pretense.

As for his unborn child… He loved that small life already, from the second he'd seen the sonogram of it, lying safely cocooned within his wife's womb.

A week after they'd reached New York, he'd broken the silence between them to announce that he'd made an appointment for her with an ob-gyn recommended to him by his personal physician. Normally, he'd have asked one of his sisters-in-law to suggest a doctor but considering that none of them knew he even had a wife, much less a pregnant one, that had been out of the question.

He'd expected Alessia to argue but she hadn't. Despite everything he knew her to be, he had to admit she seemed to have maternal instincts. She'd given up wine, ate carefully and, a couple of times, he'd seen her with one hand lying lightly over her belly.

Like the day he'd taken her for her ob-gyn appointment.

He'd stood by dutifully while she was examined, his eyes straight ahead, but his air of removal had vanished when the ultrasound technician appeared.

"Let's see what we can see," the woman had said cheerfully, and Nick's gaze had been inexorably drawn to his wife, lying on the examining table, eyes wide, her left hand forming what could only have been a protective cover over her belly.

"Move your hand, please," the tech had said and, without thinking, Nick had reached for Alessia's hand and clutched it in his.

And there it was. A black speck that was their baby.

"Excellent picture," the tech had said happily, pointing out features only she could see, and Nick had squeezed his wife's hand and she had squeezed his, and then their eyes had met and he had remembered everything, how she had lied to him with her hands, her mouth, her body…

"Hell," he growled.

Enough was enough. It was time to get his life back. See

a lawyer. Discuss his choices. Legal separation. Divorce. The ways in which they would affect his demand for custody when his child was born because, without question, he would demand it.

He would not permit his son or daughter to be raised five thousand miles away by a woman with the same duplicitous morals of her fifteenth-century ancestors. She was not fit to be a mother. What he saw now…what he *thought* he saw now—her changed diet, the hand over the belly, even the tears he'd thought had glittered in her eyes during that sonogram—

Lies, all of it. But then, lies were her specialty.

Okay. He needed to make an appointment with an attorney. Not the ones Orsini Brothers retained, not until he told his brothers about Alessia, and then he'd have to let the entire clan in on his secret and he could imagine what a mess that was bound to—

His intercom light blinked. His PA was calling. Never mind. Whatever she wanted could wait. But the light kept blinking and finally Nick cursed and reached for the phone. Even as he did, the door burst open and his sisters, Anna and Isabella, marched into the room.

Nick forced a smile.

"Hey, girls. I'm glad to see you, but it's polite to wait until—"

"We are not 'girls,'" Izzy said, in a tone that dropped the temperature fifty degrees. "We are women."

"Yeah. Right. I only meant—"

"But then, what do you know about women?" Anna said, eyes cold as ice.

"Listen," Nick said, "whatever this is, I'm not—"

"What in the bloody, holy hell do you mean by getting married and then hiding the marriage and your wife from the rest of us?"

Nick blanched. He looked past his sisters, saw his PA just behind them, saw her mouth fall open.

Say something, he thought furiously. But his mind was blank.

Instead, he strode past both Anna and Izzy. "No calls," he barked, ushering his PA out the door and slamming it after her.

"Nick," Izzy said, "we want an answer."

Izzy, normally as sweet and gentle as the flowers she loved to nurture, looked as if she wanted to slug him. Anna was breathing fire as only she could. He had a quick flash to what she'd been like as a teenager, how she'd dyed her pale blond hair black, painted her nails black, dressed in black, wore black lipstick, how she'd stood up to her brothers' teasing, their mother's hand-wringing and, most impressively, their father's fury...

"Are you deaf?" she snapped. "We were just at your place. We saw her. And we want to know—"

"What were you doing," Nick demanded, narrowing his eyes, "snooping around in my place?"

"Oh, that's perfect!" Izzy laughed with disdain. "He's going to try and lay the blame on us—but what else can you expect from a man?"

"Listen here, you two—"

"No," Anna said, tossing her blond hair out of her eyes and pointing an accusatory finger at his chest, "*you* listen! You are married. You have a wife. And you're expecting a baby."

Nick glared back. Then he let out a groan, went behind his desk and sank into his swivel chair.

"Yes."

His sisters looked at each other. Anna snorted. Izzy shook her head.

"And when," she said, "when, exactly, were you going to let the rest of the world know?"

Nick gave a strangled laugh. "I don't know. After the baby's born. After my divorce." He looked up, laughter gone, jaw flexing with tension. "Now, what were you doing at my condo?"

"We met for lunch," Isabella said. "And Anna remembered you had something for her at your place."

Nick looked blank. Anna rolled her eyes.

"I'm taking tort law this semester, remember? The day of Falco's wedding, you promised you'd give me the legal analysis from that French deal you did last year—you said you had it in your home office and if you didn't remember to courier it to me, I could just stop by if I was in the neighborhood and get it myself, but I got busy and forgot about it until now and—"

"And," Isabella said impatiently, "we were having lunch a couple of blocks from your condo, and Anna thought of that file. So, she phoned to make sure your housekeeper was in, a woman answered—"

"A woman answers," Anna said, picking up the story, "and I say, 'Hi, this is Anna Orsini,' and she says, 'Who?' and I say, 'Anna, Nick's sister, who's this?' and she says, 'This is his wife,' and then she bursts into tears!"

"Merda," Nick said, and instead of yelling at him again, his sisters saw the misery in their brother's face, looked at each other and went around the desk. They squatted beside him and each clasped one of his hands.

"Nicky," Izzy said softly, "tell us what happened."

So he told them. Everything.

Almost everything.

He left out the part about the pain lodged deep within his heart because he'd barely begun to admit that to himself. Why should a man's heart ache over a woman who was a cheat and a liar?

But he told them all the rest. How he'd thought Alessia was

an honest, good woman. How he'd discovered, by accident, that she wasn't. That she had lured him into doing what her father had wanted, lured him into more than that, into having to marry her…

They listened.

That had always been the thing about his sisters. They both knew how to listen. They never sat in judgment. Anna, maybe because she'd been judged too many times in her black hair/ black nails/black clothes/black lipstick days; Isabella, maybe because from childhood on, she'd given herself over to nurturing things that nobody else thought could be saved. They listened, and when he finally stopped talking, they sighed.

"You want my third-year, almost-ready-to-graduate-from-NYU-law-school-and-pass-the-bar, legal-eagle opinion?" Anna asked. Nick nodded, and she sighed again.

"You're screwed."

Nick looked at her. For the first time in weeks, in what felt like centuries, he laughed. Really, really laughed.

"That's your legal-eagle opinion? I hate to tell you this, kid, but if it is, you're not ready for that bar exam."

"You're screwed," his sister said softly, "because you're in love with your wife."

Nick snatched his hand from hers. "No way!"

"You're in love with her, Nicky," Isabella said, "and she's in love with you, and unless one of you comes to your senses, you're going to toss away a really good thing."

Nick jerked his hand from hers, too. A muscle knotted in his jaw.

"You don't get it," he said coldly. "Alessia Antoninni—the Princess Antoninni—is one hell of an actress. Just because she saw her chance to play another scene in this farce, just because she told you she loves me—"

Anna stood up. "What she told us was that she despises

you. That you're the most pigheaded, most stubborn, most impossible idiot she's ever met."

Nick smiled grimly. "Sure sounds like a declaration of love to me."

Isabella got to her feet, too. "Did you ever ask her to explain that conversation you overheard?"

"And hear another lie?" Nick hesitated. "Why? Did she explain it to you?"

"She didn't explain anything. She didn't tell us anything. She only said she hated you. And, Nicky, trust us. When a woman says she hates a guy the way Alessia said she hates you, what she's really saying is that she's crazy in love with him."

"That's ridiculous," Nick said, but something inside him seemed to stretch its wings. "She doesn't love me. And I don't love her. Once she's had my baby—"

"Nick," Anna said gently, "go home. Talk to your wife. Ask her to tell you what she feels about you."

"It's pointless."

Isabella smiled. So did Anna. It crossed Nick's mind that they were right, they weren't girls anymore.

"If it is," Anna said, "I know a really terrific almost-attorney who'll handle the divorce, cheap."

They blew him kisses, and then they were gone.

Nick's PA left.

His brothers hadn't been in at all that day. It was a Friday and all three had been out of town on business. They were back; Rafe and Dante had called a couple of hours ago, Falco had phoned minutes after that. All had left the same message. They'd be at The Bar at seven this evening, an old Friday-night habit, one they'd kept though they no longer stayed there longer than a couple of hours.

Nick considered stopping by for a beer. Anything to clear his head of the nonsense Anna had put into it.

No. Bad idea.

He'd tried that last week, figuring maybe it would keep him from thinking about Alessia. His brothers had spent the first hour talking about their wives and the second asking him how come he was so quiet lately and wasn't there anything new in his life?

Not a hell of a lot, he'd been tempted to say, *just a wife I don't trust, a kid I didn't plan on…*

No. He was not going to drop into The Bar.

He wasn't going to try and have a conversation with his wife, either—and he had to stop thinking of her that way. Alessia was no more his wife than she was the sweet, innocent, loving woman he'd believed her to be, he thought as he stepped from a cab outside his Central Park West condominium building.

She was exactly the cold, scheming daughter of the aristocracy he'd initially assumed her to be, and it was time to deal with reality.

Tomorrow, he'd ask a friend to recommend an attorney, meet with the guy and get his advice on how to safeguard himself and his unborn child when he divorced Alessia, which he would do as soon as the baby arrived. She could go home to Daddy or stay in the States. He'd support her; he knew his responsibilities. But his kid would be his. Entirely his. And if he had to fight for custody—

"Good evening, Mr. Orsini."

Cheerful chitchat with the doorman. It was the last thing he was in the mood for.

"George," Nick said, and started past the man.

"I hope you don't mind my asking…"

"Asking what?"

"If everything's okay, sir. With Mrs. Orsini."

Okay. George was the only other person, aside from the ob-gyn and his sisters, who knew there was a Mrs. Orsini....

Wait a minute.

Nick stood absolutely still. Then he turned toward the doorman.

"Why wouldn't it be?"

George hesitated. "Well, I just thought—I mean, I'm not prying, sir, it's just she asked me about the nearest hospital when I hailed the cab for her and—"

"Where?" Nick's voice was rough with urgency. "Where did you tell her to go?"

"I suggested she go to Mount Sinai. I know it's not the closest but—"

Nick was already on his way.

Friday nights were not the best time to be in an emergency room. The place was full of drunks and dopers and people clutching jaws and elbows and looking as if they were on their last breath.

Alessia wasn't among them.

It took Nick ten minutes to find a nurse who might know something, but only two to convince her that he would take the place apart unless she told him where he could find his wife.

Alessia had come in half an hour before, bleeding vaginally. She'd given her ob-gyn's name. The admitting nurse knew the man, knew he had staff privileges. She'd called him and he was with Alessia now, in a private room, and if Mr. Orsini would just take a seat in the waiting room...

Nick ran for the elevator, knew he'd never have the patience to wait and took the fire stairs. By the time he reached the right floor, found the right room, he was breathing hard.

Breathing hard and scared as he had never been in his life,

not in combat, not in clandestine ops, not in anything. His wife, his *wife,* was behind the door ahead of him. His wife, whom he loved with all his heart, all his soul, with everything he was or ever would be…

He dragged in a deep breath. Knocked. Turned the doorknob…

And saw his princess, pale and forlorn-looking, in an ugly hospital gown that only made her more beautiful, in a hospital bed that seemed to dwarf her.

"Alessia," he whispered.

She turned her face toward him. Her eyes lit—and then the light in them dimmed.

"Nicolo," she said. "How did you—"

He hurried to her side, grasped her cold hand in his, brought it to his lips. "What happened? Are you all right? Where's the doctor? Why didn't you call me?"

Despite the heaviness in her heart, Nicolo's rushed questions made Alessia smile.

"I am fine, Nicolo. The doctor stepped out for a moment. As for why I didn't call you…" Her smile faded. "I met your sisters today." Her voice dropped to a choked whisper. "And—and I found out that you have not told anyone about me. About us. About the baby. And I knew then that any hope I had that you would someday want me, love me—"

Nick silenced her the only way that mattered. He kissed her. Softly. Tenderly. The sweetness of her taste filled him.

"Alessia, sweetheart…I love you with all my heart. I'll always love you."

Tears filled her eyes. "You don't. You are only saying it because—"

"I'm saying it because it's true."

Alessia shook her head. "You say it because of this. The emergency. It has made you think you love me but—"

"I love you, princess. I adore you. I was just too damned

stupid to see it, or maybe too scared to put my heart in your hands."

Her eyes searched his. Some of the sadness in their blue depths seemed to fade. Nick felt his heart lift.

"Oh, Nicolo," she whispered, "I love you so much! If you knew how I have longed to hear you say that you love me, too…"

"I'm going to say it every day for the rest of our lives, baby, if you'll forgive me for having been such a fool all these weeks."

"I was the fool. I should have explained everything, but—"

"We need to talk. I know that." Nick lifted his wife's hands to his lips and kissed them. "But first tell me what happened today. What did the doctor say?"

"The baby is fine."

"Good. That's great. But you. Are you all right? Because—because I can't—I can't lose you, sweetheart. Do you understand? You're my world, my heart, my life."

His wife's smile was the most beautiful sight imaginable. "As you are mine, Nicolo. And I am fine. The doctor says I only need a few days rest."

Nick let out a pent-up breath, tilted Alessia's face to his and kissed her.

"Can you ever forgive me? When I think of how I treated you, of what I so stupidly believed—"

"No, no, it is my fault, too. I should have told you about…" Alessia took a deep breath. "My father had threatened to remove my mother from the *sanatorio* unless I met with you. But the rest—what I came to feel for you, it was all true. I fell in love with you, Nicolo, so deeply in love that I forgot to ask what he had done about my mother. The conversation you overheard was about her future. I was trying to find a way to be sure he could never hurt her again—"

"He won't," Nick said, with such stern determination that Alessia knew his words were a promise. "I'll see to it your mother is always happy and well-cared for."

"You are a good man, Nicolo Orsini," she said softly. "I know I cannot be what—what I believed you to be."

"A thug?" Nick smiled as he gathered his wife in his arms. "It's worse than that, sweetheart. I'm an investment banker."

She laughed, looped her arms around his neck and kissed him. After a long, long time, Nick drew back and framed her face with his hands.

"*Principessa*. Will you do me the honor of marrying me?"

Alessia touched the tip of her index finger to her husband's beautiful mouth. Her eyes were as bright as stars.

"But we are already married."

"I want to marry you the right way." He grinned. "A Sicilian wedding. The works. You know. The church. The reception. My brothers and their wives welcoming you to our family, my sisters driving you nuts, my mother sobbing because I've finally found the perfect *sposa*. You in a white wedding gown... and me in a tux that makes me look like something out of Madame Tussaud's."

Alessia laughed again. It was, Nick thought, the most beautiful sound he'd ever heard. Smiling, he bent his head and laid his forehead against hers.

"Is that a yes?"

She kissed him.

"It is, with all my heart, a 'yes.' Now, *mio amante, per favore,* take me home."

And, with joy filling his heart, Nick did.

EPILOGUE

SOFIA Orsini wept with joy at the news that her fourth son was taking a wife.

The civil ceremony in Italy? It did not count. They would have a real wedding in the old-fashioned Greenwich Village church Sofia loved—the church she still thought of as being part of her beloved Little Italy. The reception would be in the conservatory of the Orsini mansion. Isabella would arrange for the flowers, Anna would deal with the menu, Chiara and Gabriella and Elle would take Alessia shopping for the perfect gown. Her veil would be the one her new mother-in-law had worn so many years before.

It would be, Sofia announced, a perfect day.

And it was.

Nick couldn't seem to stop smiling. His brothers teased him about it, but then they herded him into a corner, hugged him, got teary-eyed—although, to a man, they'd have denied it—and told him how great it was to see him so happy.

"Yeah," Nick said, his smile becoming a grin, "well, you know, I couldn't let you guys leave me in the dust."

Rafe, Dante, Falco and Nicolo all laughed. Alessia heard them, looked at her husband…

The smile she gave him made him glow.

She glowed, too. And everyone agreed that the small bump

beneath the silk of her white bridal gown only added to her beauty.

"I love your family, even your father, because he brought you into my life," she told Nicolo later that afternoon, as they swayed together on the dance floor. "Your brothers are wonderful. So are their wives. And your sisters... Why are they not married?"

Anna and Isabella, on their way to the dessert table, overheard her. They flashed their new sister-in-law bright smiles but when they'd moved past her, they rolled their eyes.

"Married," Izzy said, with a snort. "I came within an inch of telling her the reason."

"Me, too." Anna looked at a silver platter of cannoli, sighed and slid first one of the rich pastries, then another, on a plate. "Why would a woman be foolish enough to tie herself down to a man?"

"Too many cannoli aren't good for you," Izzy said primly, and snatched one from Anna's plate with her fingers. "As for marriage... It's fine for Chiara and Gaby and Elle. And now for Alessia."

"But not for us," Anna said, with self-righteous conviction. "Never, ever."

Izzy licked a bit of ricotta from the tip of her pinkie. "I'll drink to that," she said, reaching for a flute of champagne.

Anna reached for one, too. *"Salute,"* she said, and the Orsini sisters touched glasses, grinned, and each drank down the fizzy stuff in one unladylike gulp.

HARLEQUIN Presents

Coming Next Month

from **Harlequin Presents® EXTRA.** Available December 7, 2010.

Coming Next Month

from **Harlequin Presents®.** Available December 28, 2010.

REQUEST YOUR
FREE BOOKS!

HARLEQUIN *Presents*

2 FREE NOVELS PLUS
2 FREE GIFTS!

PASSION
GUARANTEED
SEDUCTION

YES! Please send me 2 FREE Harlequin Presents® novels and my 2 FREE gifts (gifts are worth about $10). After receiving them, if I don't wish to receive any more books, I can return the shipping statement marked "cancel." If I don't cancel, I will receive 6 brand-new novels every month and be billed just $4.05 per book in the U.S. or $4.74 per book in Canada. That's a saving of at least 15% off the cover price! It's quite a bargain! Shipping and handling is just 50¢ per book.* I understand that accepting the 2 free books and gifts places me under no obligation to buy anything. I can always return a shipment and cancel at any time. Even if I never buy another book, the two free books and gifts are mine to keep forever.

106/306 HDN E5M4

Name _____ (PLEASE PRINT) _____

Address _____ Apt. # _____

City _____ State/Prov. _____ Zip/Postal Code _____

Signature (if under 18, a parent or guardian must sign)

Mail to the **Harlequin Reader Service:**
IN U.S.A.: P.O. Box 1867, Buffalo, NY 14240-1867
IN CANADA: P.O. Box 609, Fort Erie, Ontario L2A 5X3

Not valid for current subscribers to Harlequin Presents books.

Are you a current subscriber to Harlequin Presents books and want to receive the larger-print edition? Call 1-800-873-8635 today!

* Terms and prices subject to change without notice. Prices do not include applicable taxes. N.Y. residents add applicable sales tax. Canadian residents will be charged applicable provincial taxes and GST. Offer not valid in Quebec. This offer is limited to one order per household. All orders subject to approval. Credit or debit balances in a customer's account(s) may be offset by any other outstanding balance owed by or to the customer. Please allow 4 to 6 weeks for delivery. Offer available while quantities last.

Your Privacy: Harlequin Books is committed to protecting your privacy. Our Privacy Policy is available online at www.eHarlequin.com or upon request from the Reader Service. From time to time we make our lists of customers available to reputable third parties who may have a product or service of interest to you. If you would prefer we not share your name and address, please check here. ☐

Help us get it right—We strive for accurate, respectful and relevant communications. To clarify or modify your communication preferences, visit us at www.ReaderService.com/consumerschoice.

*Harlequin Presents® is thrilled
to introduce the first installment of
an epic tale of passion and drama by*
**USA TODAY Bestselling Author
Penny Jordan!**

*When buttoned-up Giselle first meets
the devastatingly handsome Saul Parenti,
the heat between them is explosive....*

"LET ME GET THIS STRAIGHT. Are you actually suggesting that I would stoop to that kind of game playing?"

Saul came out from behind his desk and walked toward her. Giselle could smell his hot male scent and it was making her dizzy, igniting a low, dull, pulsing ache that was taking over her whole body.

Giselle defended her suspicions. "You don't want me here."

"No," Saul agreed, "I don't."

And then he did what he had sworn he would not do, cursing himself beneath his breath as he reached for her, pulling her fiercely into his arms and kissing her with all the pent-up fury she had aroused in him from the moment he had first seen her.

Giselle certainly *wanted* to resist him. But the hand she raised to push him away developed a will of its own and was sliding along his bare arm beneath the sleeve of his shirt, and the body that should have been arching away from him was instead melting into him.

Beneath the pressure of his kiss he could feel and taste her gasp of undeniable response to him. He wanted to devour her, take her and drive them both until they were equally satiated—even whilst the anger within him that she should make him feel that way roared and burned its resentment of his need.

She was helpless, Giselle recognized, totally unable to withstand the storm lashing at her, able only to cling to the man who was the cause of it and pray that she would survive.

Somewhere else in the building a door banged. The sound exploded into the sensual tension that had enclosed them, driving them apart. Saul's chest was rising and falling as he fought for control; Giselle's whole body was trembling.

Without a word she turned and ran.

Find out what happens when Saul and Giselle succumb to their irresistible desire in

THE RELUCTANT SURRENDER

Available January 2011 from Harlequin Presents®